COTTON BLUES

Edem Awumey

Cotton
Blues

a novel

translated by
Phyllis Aronoff *and*
Howard Scott

MAWEN𝒵I
HOUSE

We acknowledge the support of the Canada Council for the Arts for our publishing program. We also acknowledge support from the Government of Ontario through the Ontario Arts Council.

We acknowledge the financial support of the Government of Canada.

Cover design by Sabrina Pignataro

Author photo by Steve Arnold

Library and Archives Canada Cataloguing in Publication

Title: Cotton blues : a novel / Edem Awumey ; translated by Phyllis Aronoff and Howard Scott.
Other titles: Noces de coton. English
Names: Awumey, Edem, 1975- author | Aronoff, Phyllis, 1945- translator | Scott, Howard, 1952- translator
Description: Translation of: Noces de coton.
Identifiers: Canadiana (print) 20240431219 | Canadiana (ebook) 20240431243 | ISBN 9781774151778 (softcover) | ISBN 9781774151785 (EPUB) | ISBN 9781774151792 (PDF)
Subjects: LCGFT: Novels.
Classification: LCC PS8601.W86 N6313 2024 | DDC C843/.6—dc23

Printed and bound in Canada by Coach House Printing

Mawenzi House Publishers
192 Spadina Ave, Suite 417
Toronto, ON, M5T 2C2
Canada

www.mawenzihouse.com

To my grandparents,

to my people on every shore.

The vultures will fight over my body,
the hyenas will suck my bare bones,
you won't be able to bury me when I die,
because all our lands have been lost.

Ouyi Tassane, *Rejaki Tangwena*

ONE DAY I'LL HAVE TO ACCEPT the fact that all I possess is a miserable body and not what you could call a land of my own, a country, a home. I looked at the photograph given to me one day by an old man in a godforsaken town somewhere in Liberia. I looked at the photograph of the scrawny, sickly body and bruised back of Samuel Brown. Samuel flogged to death by Mr James Hoogan, the disciplined overseer, one morning in the year 1850 under a beautiful sun in a cotton field of Alabama. And Samuel's son, little Abraham, is crying, clinging to the brightly coloured dress of his mother, the virtuous Winnie, who is trying to avert her eyes from the spectacle. Winnie, to whom Pastor Bill had said the day before, Samuel must accept his fate, the ways of God are inscrutable. . . . The old man who gave me the photograph said, Son, the black earth and the Black body have been and still remain the site, the terrain, the arena of acts of violence and death. For the thousandth time, I touched the image, the worn paper, Samuel Brown's back.

THE WATCH ON MY WRIST READ 12:10. My feet and hands were tied, but I was regaining my wits enough to pick up the thread of the events that had led to my being on the floor. Kerosene fumes wafted around us. Perhaps it was already the smell of the end. And from the corner where he had stuck me, I saw the man open one of the exhibition hall windows that looked out onto the street, spray fuel on a corner of a photograph he was holding at arm's length, and light it with a lighter he took from one of the pockets of his corduroy pants. Still half in a haze, my body aching from the electric shock I had received, I began to understand little by little, through a series of fleeting images, what had happened to me. The guy waited nervously for a few seconds to make sure the fire had taken before throwing the photograph to the pavement fifteen metres below. It was rush hour and a crowd of onlookers must have begun to gather outside, strollers and idlers and street vendors, fascinated or surprised, among them my old friend Ed Kaba, the museum director. And very faintly I heard Ed swear, Good God! He must have gone out for a bite, Ed, that stoic servant of this country of the Sahel, a country, he said, of weary but honest souls.

Outside, a nasty sun must be burning foreheads, smiles, and birds. From the sidewalk, Ed, who was in charge of the Museum of the Green Revolution, which had just opened in the capital, spoke to the man standing at the window contemplating the charred remains of the photograph on the pavement. Ed the bureaucrat, who I guessed was in a panic, sweating the sweat of tragedy, shouted, What have you done,

Old Toby? This is very serious! I'm calling the police! And why did you turn off your phone and take out your earphones? . . . And from my position as the prisoner on the floor behind the guy standing looking out on the street, I imagined my friend taking out his phone and beginning a conversation with the cops, making expansive, emphatic gestures. The man at the window, however, maintained an astonishing calm, a placid prophet in the eye of the storm. He shouted, I don't care about your miserable photos and I won't talk on the phone; I want the whole world to hear me! What he wanted was reparations, compensation. Two hundred million francs is what we're demanding from The Firm! They swindled us with their bad cotton! Two hundred million, or else I'll burn every one of these magnificent photographs! The photographs, and especially, my hostage! So hurry up and do something! Contact the pirates from The Firm and tell them to get a move on! There, I'm sending you a text with the bank information. You transfer me the money, I'll check it from here and we'll be quits!

I gave a start, but then I persuaded myself the guy was bluffing, that, on the contrary, it was in his interest to keep me alive. And in a vain attempt to push away the idea of impending death, I focused my attention on the photographs he wanted to incinerate. They were signed by a certain Jean Lenoir, and in the hours to come were supposed to be revealed to the public with great fanfare. Discovering them a little over an hour ago, I had observed that, as Ed had told me a few days before—and it had piqued my interest, or I wouldn't have thrown myself into this quagmire—the series of photographs of workers in our countryside was indeed titled "The Peasant Dance," a title that, as noted in the exhibition text, was borrowed from Pieter Bruegel, known as the Elder, the painter of the flat Flemish countryside. Bruegel brought back to life in West Africa. The central theme of the photographs was the peasants' happiness, a naive, grotesque epiphany of the green land, its men and its fruits. A weird project, Ed Kaba had warned me, adding, But, dear friend, I, a loyal citizen, have been entrusted with the management of our Museum of the Green

Revolution. Come over if you're getting bored in your retreat on the coast, grab a plane and come see me in my city of the Sahel. I'll give you a scoop, you'll see these photographs by a joker making fun of our peasants. Come and admire that clownish laughter displayed on the walls. . . . I had some idea who Jean Lenoir was. As a regular visitor to museums and exhibitions, I had once read a paper on his work, he was a Breton adventurer who claimed to have Africa and its pathetic Black riffraff in his body and soul. And Ed said he'd been paid handsomely by The Firm to crisscross the countryside for a ridiculously short week, armed with his craziness and with costumes and headgear from another century to dress up his models, and knickknacks and cardboard for the scenery, giving them this order: Smile, smile, you're so awkward!

THE AIR STILL SMELLED OF KEROSENE and disaster. In my corner, my limbs aching, rage in my belly, and impatient death hanging over my head, I tried to forget by thinking about the photograph that had been burned. An uninspired conventional shot of a pastoral world, happy peasants in a setting of adobe huts with straw roofs, kids with round bellies and laughing faces playing in the dust around the withered legs of an elder smoking his pipe, two equally radiant women pounding millet or sorghum in front of the neighbouring hut, while, further away, at the edge of the village, a group of weary men empty their day's harvest into a multilevel granary from big burlap bags. It was, as I could see, incredibly trite, and you couldn't say it was a great loss for humanity that the man had burned the photograph and thrown it into the street among the flies and the wretched dogs. Rather, he had done a service to the art of photography by expunging from our view that scene of dubious and unremarkable happiness, like the vast majority of the hundred or so photographs collected there in the inaugural exhibition of the Museum of the Green Revolution.

The guy stood at the window for a brief moment. He was as thin as a skeleton, an odd character, like a saint in agony. Over his grey corduroy pants he was wearing a shirt in a print of birds against a grey sky, yes, a guy covered with birds, and it must have been the hornbills and swallows on his torso that gave him his nerve. The hair on his bare arms was white, like the goatee that extended his pointed chin, and he had a narrow nose, a rather wide forehead, and a bald head like that of a vulture that has suffered the rigours of poor seasons. But he was not quite over the hill, Old Toby, I would guess sixty years old at most. On his feet, running shoes, clean new black Nikes. He moved away from the window, turned around, and, catching me looking at his wonderful shoes, said, American Nikes, very comfortable, that's one thing I can still stand. As for the rest, those Yankees from The Firm are cheats! If they don't pay, it will be my pleasure to reduce these ridiculous photographs to ashes. You saw the title of this sham of an exhibition, huh? Yes, I answered hesitantly, wondering what part of my body he was going to burn first, what piece of skin the torture would begin with. Toby continued, A bad joke, "The Peasant Dance." Not a soul dances in our fields. And what an idea, a Museum of the Green Revolution!

I answered that I too failed to see in this country anything that could justify devoting a museum to the rotten fruits of any revolution, green, pink, or blue. A travesty! he replied, beginning to take another forced smile down from the wall, We remained poor peasants, and to finish us off, they stuck us with their damn genetically modified cotton. . . . From the street, Ed Kaba barked again, Release my friend, stop all this and give yourself up, Toby! The cops are coming and, believe me, they aren't going to do you any favours! No! replied Toby, I have nothing to lose. Over his face passed the shadow of an old sadness.

He dropped to the floor beside the window with a horrible cracking sound of the remains of his worn bones, and, his eyes fixed on a distant horizon, began talking to an invisible person, an attentive ghost, This is it, Ruth. I've taken action. Pray for me. Or call for reinforcements from the gods we were with those nights in Georgia. What news from Savannah? What news of the gloomy, century-old oak in Chippewa Square you said you like to sit under and daydream? And of Zeke the madman who paces Factors Walk reciting the same verse of the Bible over and over? What echoes from the city of all the ghosts? I dream, my dear Ruth, I dream of your skin. I also wanted to tell you that my exhibition will be beautiful. If only you could see it.

And while I unobtrusively twisted my wrists and ankles, trying to loosen my bonds—no way was I going to die here!—he started rummaging in a huge worn leather bag against the wall on my left. He took out a slingshot of old wood polished by long use. The elastic and the leather that held the projectile seemed solid, so I thought it was not a museum piece but one that Toby must often have used. However, he said, It's not mine, I've never been able to shoot at birds. Yes, maybe I'm a sensitive soul. The slingshot belonged to Boula, a friend, a grower who has since disappeared. We, his friends, looked for him in vain in the savannahs and here in town. We discovered that he'd taken some things with him, so we thought he'd gone south to the coast and must be working as a docker in some port now. Boula held on to the slingshot after he lost everything. His new field of genetically modified cotton only produced a thin grey fibre, so he had to sell the few animals he had left, some rickety furniture, moth-eaten wool fabric, and fake gold jewellery to pay off his debts. But, you know, that wasn't enough! Maybe you won't believe me, but in the end he had nothing left to eat. So he hunted birds. Early in the morning, you'd see him running all over the countryside, alone, swearing and shooting birds, which he would stuff into a big pouch slung across his chest. And in the evening he would eat the birds. Some days, he wasn't so lucky and came to beg a few coins from me. Until he couldn't stand it any more. He didn't take the slingshot with him, it probably wouldn't be of any use where he is now.

Shit, impossible to undo my bonds! Toby went back to his bag and took out a hammer and some nails. He hammered a nail into the wall between two of the photographs of the exhibition and hung the slingshot there, saying it was the first item in his own exhibition. . . . The old man in that town in Liberia where I had gone to do a news story told me, This is a photograph of the killing of my great-grandfather, Samuel Brown. You can keep it and show it if you want. I got it from my father. The photographer wrote the name of the overseer on the back and quietly passed it to Samuel's little son Abraham, who is none

8

other than my grandfather, and who as an adult ran away to Liberia as soon as he could. It seems he no longer wanted to harvest cotton, he wanted to put his skin to some other use. He didn't give a damn about the land, because it never belonged to anyone.

47

12:21 PM. MY TEETH CLENCHED, I cursed that Toby. He glared at me and said he was in deep shit. I don't see why I should back down now, young man, he said calmly, and repeated, I have nothing to lose. He said that again and again while he nervously circled the room, prowling like a wounded animal in the exhibition hall with its white walls and purple floor, ready to do battle with all the devils and the men who had cheated him, and there I was, sitting on the purple cement for some unimaginable reason, pondering my misadventure, which in the beginning was supposed to be an instructive and pleasant experience during my summer break from my work as a freelance journalist running around the dying world and its feverish streets. I had been back from Berlin for a week, back in my city, Le Port, the capital of the country, with its feet in the Atlantic, where I'd met Ed twenty years ago, in 1994, when we were students. Ed Kaba was from the neighbouring country, and his parents, expatriates in my country on the coast, were doing business in everything, fabrics, furniture, spare parts, like many of their nomadic fellow-citizens who had emigrated south fleeing the droughts and the crickets. We spent three intense years at the lycée skipping physics classes, competing in races, helping in his parents' warehouse at the end of the day for small wages that we would immediately spend on clothes and movies. After my graduation and departure for Berlin, Ed and I stayed in contact, he studying economics at university in his country, where his parents had finally returned, while I was still searching for my path.

I remembered talking to my friend on the phone three months before, about my last investigation, which had fallen through because the contacts and the sources I was counting on had suddenly chickened out. I was in the Indian countryside in Rajasthan, trying to write a piece on the suicides by debt-strapped peasants. I had obtained testimony from growers, although nothing more than what was already known, unfortunately. But I had a card up my sleeve, three broken souls who had worked with The Firm and who were ready to pour out their sorrows, with supporting evidence. I had returned empty-handed to my sad Berlin lair. When I told him the story of that magnificent fiasco, Ed Kaba had not commented but had just renewed his invitation to come see the exhibition of the century in his city.

And as soon as I got off the plane, I went to the museum, where Ed let me look at those bloody photographs before the arrival of the officials and the mad and the sane people of the city who had been invited to the vernissage. For more than an hour, I studied and photographed the pictures of happy peasants displayed before my delighted eyes in different formats. Ed told me before leaving me alone that security reinforcements would soon arrive. He added, I should mention that we had a disagreement with the security company over the contract, and also, the guy who assists Toby in his duties is sick and didn't show up today. So, my friend, for the time being—and I realize we're taking a risk—our precious photographs are being watched over only by Toby, the guardian angel I hired a while ago.

The obnoxious angel doing his rounds in the hall had greeted me with a stiff smile and said grudgingly, You're the director's friend? Well, you're privileged. And he continued pacing up and down, a solitary sentry, while I took out my notebook and camera to use before others arrived. I observed that he compulsively consulted his watch, nervous as if he was afraid of missing the appointment of his miserable life. He became increasingly nervous as it got closer to noon. And after twelve o'clock chimed from the steeple of a church a few streets away and I had started going back through my notes and photos, he went over to the exits of the main exhibition hall and locked them. He first locked the double doors of the main entrance, then the two emergency exits on the sides, taking care to block the springs. I wondered if whoever he was expecting would miraculously materialize in the middle of the hall or if a ball would take place behind the closed doors. He came over to me, looking annoyed, and said, Sorry, friend, if you could have finished your explorations before noon. Now it's too late. You'll be my witness and the guarantor of my survival in this place. . . . And scarcely had he spoken these words when he turned a Taser on me. I was thrown to the floor, my brain frozen and my muscles defeated, useless. Looking me in the eye, he said, The situation was serious. And besides, I shot at you from quite far away, you're hardly shaken! But all things considered, it's not a bad thing to have a front-row seat for what is to come, it seems you were born to get the scoop on events, you must have a gift for being in the middle of the great moments of history. And you won't be bored! Assuming that you stay alive, that is.

Still wondering how I would be able to extricate myself, I turned my head to the side, towards the back wall of the hall, where the largest photograph was hanging, which must have measured at least a metre and a half by ninety centimetres, a ridiculous pastiche in which the photographer had recreated in his own style Bruegel's *Peasant Dance*, an oil painting on wood showing the revels of peasants in a street and village square with a glowing sky above the thatched roofs. In the photograph, all in warm colours, a group of peasants holding hands are dancing the farandole, others are drinking out of bowls, while a flute player is knocking himself out trying to play while taking part in the celebrations and two lovers in a very awkward position are kissing behind the drinkers, who are having a lively conversation around a high wooden table; in the background, a church, from which the saints of the harvest must be watching approvingly over the festivities. What amazed me in the photograph was the immaculate white headwear of the Black women, a kind of wimple out of the Middle Ages. On closer examination, you couldn't see in the faces any of the joy that would have given rise to a desire to prance around, but it might have been the intent of both the Flemish painter and the photographer to show that these people are dancing even though they don't have much, or that they're so miserable, the only thing they have left is to get drunk and screw young women, with heaven's blessing.

46

MY HEAD BURNING AND MY BACK STIFF and painful, I shot invisible projectiles at my kidnapper's head. He coughed and said, Before their bloody Bt cotton, we didn't have much, but we weren't unhappy, we weren't worn-out shadows like we are now. . . . His family had nothing, but that had never been a tragedy. In the 1970s, when the boy was growing up—according to his birth certificate, he had become a wretched Earthling one day in April 1965—his father had toiled season after season on the land of Antonin Martian, a native of Auvergne who had refused to return home after the country's independence in 1960. Toby's father had come from the north of the colony in 1956 and had been hired by Martian, who needed workers. But that gentleman paid the unfortunate native people starvation wages. That was still better than his peers who, after despoiling the Blacks of their lands, imposed forced labour on them by the crack of a whip. Toby said his father had never been a rebel, so Monsieur Antonin would have had no reason to smash his head with a hammer or flay him alive. My father was an ass, said Toby.

While Toby was confiding in me as if I were an old acquaintance rather than a stranger, the condemned man who wanted him dead, I wondered what this whole crazy situation was about. The inauguration of the museum was supposed to take place at 7 PM sharp and Toby, a hunted animal yet calm, continued walking back and forth, while from the street Ed Kaba tried to get him to engage in dialogue, using a megaphone because Toby had refused to talk on the phone.

At one point, Toby went back to the window and said to Ed, My hostage, your dear journalist friend whose visit you told me about, Mister Director, is quite compliant. But it's nearly half an hour since I made my statement, and still nothing! I repeat: if you don't pay the two hundred million, I'm going to burn your friend along with all these lovely photos of perfectly happy peasants!

He left the window, returned to his booty—me—and looked me in the eye challengingly. But what are you doing here? he asked as if he had just noticed an undesirable object on the floor against the wall. Or perhaps his unspoken question was, Where did you get the bizarre idea of coming and wasting your time in this hall, my friend, wearing out your eyes in front of those ridiculous photos? Yes, that was it, the mute question Toby was asking me, and I knew only too well why I had been so drawn to those photographs based on Bruegel. Actually I had, in spite of myself, felt an idiotic sadness and nostalgia looking at the pictures of those happy country folk; something perverse in the images reminded me of my grandfather, with whom I grew up on the plateaus, my hands clinging to his worn clothing. My German grandfather, who one morning under a sad sun, while he was washing his brushes, asked me, So, my lad, do you know Bruegel? Well, he was a great painter who gave us, among other works, *The Peasant Dance*. I discovered him one day in Bremen when I was leafing through a book on great oil paintings on wood. That was before God called me in a frighteningly clear dream to become a pastor, that is, his worker. I've travelled many roads since then, and I landed in this unhappy country of the Bight of Benin one morning in June 1947. Promise me you'll one day go see that painting in Vienna? I myself went to see it, and I believe I sensed in the gaze of the people Bruegel painted the truth about the peasants, the truth that existed before machines and all those products altered, or I should say destroyed, their labour. So here, between leading prayer sessions and religious services, I too try to paint these fields that surround us, these plateaus and their people.

Yes, those photographs reminded me of Grandfather, of all the times I went to see *The Peasant Dance* in Vienna, of the harsh judgment of my grandmother, who, to form my mind, said with a sigh, That old German man told you for the hundredth time his story of peasants celebrating on a piece of painted wood! She added that she was not sure her husband had any talent for painting, but at least it kept the old pastor busy. In fact, Grandfather Hans toiled every afternoon on his drawings and watercolours, aiming to put down on canvas a joyful, typically tropical peasant dance. In the mid-1980s, when I was going on seven years old, Grandmother said to me, In the beginning, I mean after 1948, the year we met, he did scenes from memory, of markets, bush taxi stations, or fruit picking, he drew the laughter and the actions he saw. However, he wasn't satisfied, he said the truth was not there, that what he had created was only a pale reflection of what he felt he had seen. So he changed his approach, now carrying large sheets of paper to a public square, a roadside, or the middle of the fields. But he would come back even more disappointed, and grumble about the merchants, passersby, and peasants pressed into service as models, who would freeze or try to look different and put on artificial smiles as soon as they noticed that he was drawing them, while their feet, shod in crude, thick sandals cut from tires retrieved from tractors and other machines abandoned in the fields by the Cotton Company of the colony, trod on the ferns and corkwood tree shoots on trunks lying on the ground.

For more than an hour, I remained there in that hall, ridiculous, immersed not in the artificial worlds displayed but in my own pathetic memories, films of another time with worn-out characters, an old German pastor haunted by Bruegel who wanted to capture nature and men on the blank paper, his brush pointed towards the sky and his fingers stained blue, red, and orange, and his muse who tenderly made fun of him. And Toby, armed with a lighter, came close to my bare arm. The fire hadn't yet bitten into my skin when I shouted, Stop, I have nothing to do with this! Samuel Brown groaned, Pity! The flame was ten centimetres from me when Ed Kaba reacted, Don't touch my friend! Toby laughed, Oh yeah, why shouldn't I? —We're working actively to establish contact with The Firm, Toby. So don't do anything crazy! —It's your friends from The Firm who drove me crazy! I repeat, Two hundred million or your buddy will croak! . . . When the whip burned his body, Samuel had long known that he had nothing to offer to save his skin, and Winnie cried because she had the same thought.

45

NO, I WON'T CROAK! I'd give my precious memories to get out of this jam, I said to myself, struggling against my bonds, the unrelenting pain in my body increasing my desire to attack Toby. He performed a ritual that I found strange and bizarre until I realized how ingenious it was. From a travel bag leaning against the wall he took out a kerosene lamp and lit it. He set it down on the floor behind him where it was visible through the window. In front of the lamp, he placed a plastic bottle he had taken out of the same bag. A disturbing smell of kerosene filled the room when he opened the bottle. He said, If the cops shoot me from the street, I'll fall on it, and with this little wick burning, you can guess what will come next. He lit two more lamps, and more bottles of kerosene appeared, which he placed in front of the three exits from the hall: the main door in the centre of the inner wall facing the street, and the emergency exits on the two sides. We were encircled by the flames of hell created by Toby's hands with their long, slender fingers. Everything should be okay if no one screws up, he said, I've placed the lamps at a reasonable distance from the flammable liquid. He sat down against the wall, stretched out his legs, put his hands together behind his vulture head, and closed his eyes for several long seconds, murmuring a prayer before what was to be my execution. He was facing me, a bit to one side, three metres to the left of the window. His arrangements, the invention of a reckless child or an evil magician, I said to myself with a shiver, could work, as ridiculous as they were. I ran my eyes over the photographs hanging on the walls. I had familiarized myself with some of them, especially the dozen or so I found the most successful, moments of laughter in market squares or in the fields, in which cunning, mischievous life seemed to smile on the peasants. The approach was far from trite, it seemed that those scenes, unlike the others, were candid shots. The light on the faces or on the walls of the huts, whether controlled or sensitively exploited, was beautiful. I had noted the titles of those photographs, which stood out from the rest as if to introduce doubt into the travesty, and in my corner I prayed that Toby would not target them. The aim of the exhibition, Ed had pointed out without concealing the note of irony, was to put the peasants back at the forefront of development.

I don't believe, Toby commented, leafing through a brochure touting the event, that the peasants of this continent have ever been at the forefront except for the very brief time in the seventies when a first plan for the Green Revolution, which was poorly designed, was initiated by the Rockefeller Foundation to increase agricultural production. It failed because the growers here were not into intensive monoculture. Back in the seventies when my obedient father was still Monsieur Antonin's fool—but I didn't realize that, I admired my father, I always admired him—the master had promised him a piece of land of about one hectare if he gave him at least ten years of good and loyal service. He had made that promise to the only one of his vassals who never grumbled. But it had already been a good fourteen years that my father had been toiling. That's the way it was in those days, only fools could be rewarded with a ridiculous little patch of land. And I couldn't say that the master, his wife, and their twin girls—who, like me, were ten years old at the time—were malicious; I joined in the little girls' games, and when the master came and saw me polishing his shoes, he would say mysteriously, gazing off into the distance at his Black fools taking beatings in the fields, that the growers in our part of the country would not soon want to grow more than what they needed to fill their bellies, that ambition wasn't in their genes. That I should not count on their worn-out arms and lazy ways to succeed if ever I should feel the desire to farm the land, that, furthermore, he had plans for me. Yes, my little Toby, the day I leave this place—because it's obvious that I will, although I remain attached to this land, to this goddamn country, I'm afraid of being caught in the pervasive stupidity and idleness—I'll take you with me. And there, in Auvergne, you'll be my major-domo. You'll write lovely letters to your family to lift their spirits and increase their ardour, which have been diminished by a century of colonization. However, I can do nothing about it. But forget about the land, Toby. Those were Monsieur Antonin's words, and I didn't understand then that he was taking the land from me. While a strange character ran through the fields, Old Yambo, a corporal and rifleman back from the Second Western War—it couldn't be a world war, said the old man, I didn't see why a Black man like me should have to fight. He had come back, it was said, with a bullet in his head that had driven him mad. Old Yambo, armed with a hoe, putting earth in little plastic bags gathered here and there, Yambo piling up the bags in his backyard, Yambo industrious and hurried, who always greeted you with the same words, I've got to get busy, because the earth is going away!

44

THE VOICE THAT SUDDENLY BOOMED from the megaphone startled us. I am Commissioner Wali Shango. Toby, the most sensible thing to do would be to free your hostage and come out of that building. . . . Toby opened his eyes, dragged himself to the window on his bum, and said without showing himself, Very funny, Commissioner! You don't really think I'm going to obey the first order that comes from a megaphone? —You have no choice! Wali Shango replied, the building is surrounded. Where do you think you can go? Look, Toby, you have no way out. Give yourself up and perhaps the courts will be lenient. —So we're on a first-name basis? You're not very polite, Commissioner. Seems to me you and I didn't herd cattle or sheep together in the savannahs. So your familiarity is out of place. But if you wish, why not talk like old friends. Let me hasten to assure you that I'm not going to vacate the premises. You'll have to carry me out feet first. However, if you try to shoot me, if you dare, this lovely brand-new building will go up in flames. A beautiful fire like you've rarely seen.

Shango didn't answer, and Toby closed his eyes again, displaying a deceptive calm that contrasted with the agitation he had just shown, and I was afraid he really was capable of creating carnage, burning towns and skins. He went on, continuing the monologue he had started earlier, saying to his ghost, I'm going to do it, Ruth. Meanwhile, let me guess how you spent your day . . . Not much? Well, you have to get moving! Ah! if you could only see the pieces in my museum.

He went into his bag again, and this time took out some stones, the clean, smooth ones you find in riverbeds. He said he had picked them up at his friend Boula's home along with the slingshot. On days when birds were rare in the sky of the savannahs, Boula would sit on the doorstep of his house and shoot stones into the wind and then run and pick them up in the dust and dead grass a hundred metres away. On those days, this guy who used to always have a joke ready was taciturn; I'd go see him and he wouldn't answer my questions, avoiding my gaze because he didn't want me to see the shame, the failure in his eyes. In silence he would play with the pebbles in his palm, counting them and shaking them, all he had left now was the sound of those stones. Sometimes a hummingbird would perch on the edge of the roof of his shack and taunt him, Catch me if you can, catch me, loser!

Toby put the stones in a little jute bag, which he hung on another nail, beside the slingshot. And he said that when The Firm compensated him, he would come back to town and buy one of the abandoned buildings on the old streets in the centre, a nice brick building for his museum. Then he would travel around to the peasants in the country gathering pieces for his permanent collection. He would also try to obtain sound recordings of growers telling their stories handed down from father to son, which were often very different from those in books. They would talk to him, and he would record them and take notes. They would tell of their work with hoe, machete, or daba, and the days of peanut-sorting machines, draft animals, animal-drawn carts and seed drills, cultivators, and harrows pulled by donkeys.

His grower friends could come into town any time to help him out, he said. They'll come out of the last thickets outside town and fill the streets and squares. I see them from here, excited, eager, fearless. Some thirty wretches, their muscles tense and their will unshakeable. Among them, Rana, the woman who stood at the entrance to The Firm for a whole week without being received. Is that the way to treat a lady? Malick, who started a hunger strike that he had to end on day ten because he realized that our authorities would let him croak without lifting a finger. But I told him, Malick, it's because you love this goddamn life. Also Kalo, the goatherd, who made the decision to immolate himself in front of the offices of The Firm with one of his animals, but went back on that decision because, he said, he should have asked the opinion of the poor goat he was going to sacrifice. And it's certain that Fouss, whose nickname is Lazybones because he's never farmed a single hectare, would come with them so as not to miss the fun! Yes, my buddies may very well come here, but meanwhile those people outside had better get a move on. Where's that lighter anyway? . . . The little flame was again about to lick my skin, its crazed orange tongue five centimetres from my pores. Stop, Toby! I yelled, and Ed Kaba, angry, shouted, Stop messing around, Toby! Promise me you won't touch your hostage! And Shango shouted, Cut it out, Toby! You're digging yourself in deeper! Toby yelled, I'm getting impatient! I want the money right now! We're working on it! Ed answered, And don't wreck the exhibition! That would be a disaster. And the same word crossed Winnie's lips in front of Samuel's bloodied body. She felt that what was happening before her eyes was a terrible disaster, but that there would be others, slavery was a great work that would endure over time. Winnie got it right, slavery was a masterwork, perhaps the magnum opus of a civilization.

43

THE CLOCK READ 12:43. I was still among the living, and the distant sound of what must have been the air conditioning suddenly stopped. Toby froze, pondering. It seems they've cut off our cool air. Or else the system is acting up again, as it often does. Because they can't try to get me this way while you're here. They won't take that risk. So it's a breakdown. You must have noticed that I only opened one section of the window shutter part-way to talk with the people outside, which only has a minor effect on the efficiency of the air conditioning. But now it's been cut off. I, for one, tolerate the heat quite well, and various other inconveniences. And you? —I'll croak in the next hour if that damn machine doesn't start up again! I replied. —I see, said Toby, you're as fragile as a newborn baby. —You mustn't exaggerate. But I can't do anything about it. —Try not to think about it. —Impossible.

Toby turned to the window and said to Ed Kaba and Commissioner Shango, There's a lack of cool air, gentlemen. For myself, it's not a problem, but if you want the person I'm holding to survive, you'd better check it out right away! He returned to the middle of the room. My guts twisting with fear, hoping to delay my execution, I asked him outright, Who are you, Old Toby, and who is Ruth? He stared at me for an instant and said, Ruth is none of your business. And don't call me Old Toby! This year of 2015, I registered fifty cycles on my biological counter, but that's no reason to take me for your grandfather. Let's just say that the troubles of the last four years have worn me out a bit. He paused for a minute and then said that back in the mid-1990s he had been working at the American Cultural Centre in the capital. He had refused to take over the family farm in the savannahs in the heart of the country, having seen clearly how cotton had worn his father out since those insects and other pests had proliferated and were devouring the young plants. He didn't see why his pigheaded father had to kill himself working like that, accumulating debts and ruining what strength he had left, a stubborn worker caught up in the tyrannical cycle of hard labour and meagre harvests that forced you to work more than ever the following season, a galley slave on the deck of a leaky tub doomed to sink. Toby had held out against his father's repeated calls that he take over the farm, saying, You're not a farmer anymore, Father. On the contrary, you've become a medieval vassal subject to the orders of an unseen lord. But the old man would say that cotton was the whole history of their family, the very meaning of their insignificant existence.

Toby resisted the appeals of the father and the fibre until the day when, working as a librarian, he opened a box of new books and discovered a volume promoting genetically modified cotton and the countless advantages related to its production. He said that was when his troubles began, that he hadn't been unhappy in his job as librarian, which he had obtained after getting his master's degree in English in 1990. He continued, I should have stayed behind my counter reading and lending books by Steinbeck, Faulkner, Alex Haley, Mark Twain, and other writers to lovers of fine prose. However, the temptation of the land was there, and I didn't hate working with cotton, or let's say I had finally come to like it, since 1986, when Monsieur Antonin fell ill and had to return to Aurillac for treatment. He couldn't be saved, however, so that year my father, who had been holding the fort, became the master. He was able to manage the farm, having known the suppliers, the workers, and the various buyers Monsieur Antonin had dealt with for a long time. It must also be said that in 1976, after twenty years of good and loyal service, twenty years of servility, during which I despised my father, Monsieur Antonin had finally given him the promised parcel of land, the hectare of dandelions, shrubs, and scrawny trees, on which, as the times became more prosperous—and he shared the revenues from the farm with the master's widow—he built a house. So we were able to move out of the outbuildings of the owners' house. Otherwise, on paper, the rest of the land belonged to the Auvergne man; the widow and the daughters, who had gone back to France, would came back every third year to wander there, melancholy and wondering, What are we going to do with all this? Sell it? But that's not what our poor father would have wanted, he loved this place. . . . Toby said that the widow had remained attached to the land. The last he'd heard, however, an investor from the Orient was interested. He said there was a time when the farm was profitable, adding, Cotton paid for my studies, and when you're an only son, you end up giving in to your parents since you are all they have to rely on. So one day in 2010, Toby had resigned from his job as a librarian. His superior, disappointed, had said, The land feeds us, but it can be mean too, it's a capricious, unpredictable mistress. At least, you can manage books; no one has ever been able to tame the land. But good luck, my friend! However, since your entire future is at stake, it's obvious that counting on luck would be crazy.

42

TOBY CONTINUED HIS STORY while I struggled against my bonds and the pain in my body persisted, but in order to forget my sore muscles and twisted back, I had to focus on the words of my jailer, on his memories of the people he was bringing to life. He told me his father was as happy as a child getting a present when Toby arrived at the farm with his city-dweller's junk crammed into the yellow Beetle he himself had given his son four years earlier with money from the cotton. Toby had lost his mother—may the land be as light upon her as a breeze, he murmured—ten years before. The fault, he said, staring at the white ceiling of the exhibition hall with its billions of dots, the fault of one of those nasty, tenacious, unforeseen ills the body can come up with. But I must say Mother didn't spare herself in the fields either, searching for dead wood and tracking down the awful caterpillars that eat leaves. He sighed and added that his old joker of a father had been quick to die three months after Toby took over the farm. He had expired in the fields, a dramatic heart attack as in those theatrical scenes when a lead character expires with his useless hand clutching his heart. The old man hadn't had time to pass on his secrets, tricks, and gris-gris to counter the vagaries of the cotton, he had only whispered, The land is a promise, Toby. Make a miracle of it.

Toby stood up again and studied me. He looked a bit older than his fifty years, but he was not completely decrepit. I'm no weakling, he said, you'd better believe it! He was going to use the last of his strength in the battle to come, the wild energy he had never spared, either at work or, he said smiling, with a young lady clinging to him in a discotheque under the stars in the capital, where he'd gone every Friday night at the wheel of the Beetle. And in the night of the city, they called him the Master of Rhythm, because no one could compete with him on the dance floor, where they played the fiery compositions of the Buena Vista Social Club of Havana over and over. Or else it was because the star dancer who could snatch his date from him hadn't yet been born and, he said with a conspiratorial wink—perhaps I was no longer the hostage to be executed—the beauties of the tropical night would wait impatiently for him to come down from his farm every Friday, although he had never felt the desire to go further than the odd adventure that would allow him to remain free and solitary as a bird. —I was a very strange bird! he added. A bold sea hawk. Well, until Ruth. —Who is Ruth, Toby? He paused. —Ruth, that's another story, one of those that lie in wait and take you by surprise.

And he continued the story of his wild nights possessed by the languid melodies of Ibrahim Ferrer. —Have you ever been in Cuba at a real salsa concert? he asked. —No, I've never been to Cuba, I answered. . . . I recalled Grandmother saying she had never gone beyond the limits of our part of the country, back in the eighties when, after school, I'd follow her in her daily tour of our modest orchards and gardens, while Grandfather laboured over his umpteenth canvas on the easel in front of the house, facing the mountains. We'd stop for a moment to observe the artist's work, and Grandmother would pretend to appreciate the emerging masterpiece, but Grandfather wasn't fooled, and he would mutter between his teeth, On your way, woman, or I'll lose the spark of inspiration! But aren't I your inspiration? Grandmother would retort. . . . We'd leave him there, lost in the canvas he was painting, his free hand—the right, he was left-handed—stroking his long white beard, staining it with colours that made him look like a horrible clown.

Once, as we were walking away, Grandmother revealed that in the beginning, Grandfather hadn't painted. Until the late 1940s, she said, when he confessed to his second vocation, he only did charcoal drawings of the nature around us. They were nice, but sad, with something not quite right when he drew a sombre sapote, papaya, or breadfruit tree with dull bark, or birds flying in a dreary sky. He did that until I told him it wasn't enough to draw this country and its nature only in charcoal. It was an insult, I said again and again. For months I hammered at him with that old song, until one morning when the sky was cloudy, he dared to do his first sketch with a little more colour, just a little, like a child venturing onto unfamiliar territory. He did some very simple variations on the theme of the different seasons, three paintings depicting the fields of the Colonial Cotton Company. The first was in the colours of the ochre earth with buds barely appearing; in the second, the entire canvas was covered with the intense green of growing plants; and in the last one, the brown of open cotton bolls offered the white fibre for the delectation of the gods. They weren't bad, but I told him they played into the hands of the colonists who had forced us to intensify cotton and palm nut monoculture, that what he had painted scarcely represented all the colours around us! It was not us! And I urged him to go around the little fields of taro and sorrel, the lemon trees, and the peppers that went from the orangish and green of the bird pepper to the devastating red of the nedungo.

IT WAS ALMOST 1 PM, THE HEAT was spreading through the place, I was going to die soon. In the photograph that never left my mind, the heat and the whip were burning Samuel Brown's back and he was wondering what complicated figure the overseer wanted to engrave on it, because it was long, that masterpiece of cuts, furrows, and pathways he was creating to plant his feet and flag firmly in. Toby came back to me with a small transistor radio he had dug out of his bag. He turned it on, pulled out the antenna, played with a dial, and managed to pick up a news station. He said, I love this gadget, which was my father's. On the farm, he had no problem picking up the stations, unlike cellphone networks that go in and out, fleeting and unstable. Usually I don't listen to the bullshit in the news, I put on the nostalgia station and I binge on those beautiful songs of the old days. Rumba, salsa, blues, and jazz. Have you ever listened to our fabulous jazzmen from the US South? Freddie Keppard, Buddy Bolden, and that big burly guy from New Orleans, Fats Domino? Have you ever moved to swing, bebop, free jazz? No? Don't tell me you're that uncultured? Couldn't you at least lie out of pride? I'm sure you're not a bad guy. Well, apart from jazz and a few odds and ends, America has given us nothing but misery. You think I'm exaggerating? I must admit that, these last few months, listening to old jazz has helped me put up with my troubles as an improvised cotton grower. That's the proof that we've returned to the days of slavery: like the slaves of old, all we growers have left to hold on to is music and faith. But there are limits, aren't there? . . . And he told me that he had made the decision to wreak havoc in the museum three days ago. But he had been mulling over the idea for weeks.

He was talking, but I wasn't listening to him, or rather, I was trying not to pay attention to what he was saying, I didn't want to fall into the trap of his words, which were trying to win me over to his cause and make me forget that I was hurting. I brought my knees up to my chest to create a barrier to the words. I didn't want to listen to him anymore; staying focused on my pain would sustain my outrage. I shouted that his issue had nothing to do with me. That it was doomed from the start. The Firm won't pay up, I said, because some poor grower starts burning a few photographs. And I just want to get out of here! You're wasting your time acting alone, Toby! —I don't need your opinion, he retorted. Stop bugging me! It seems to me that, up to now I've been really fair to you. That I've been magnanimous. Even if it's obvious to me that in order to make myself heard I'll have to finish you off. But meanwhile, you'll just have to put up with this, to listen and watch. —What for? I asked. —You'll be able to tell the story afterwards, if we get out of this alive. —You said it, Toby, if we get out of this. —So don't you believe in anything? Have you lost faith? —Toby, I don't know what faith is. Has hoping and praying to all the gods, known and unknown, done you any good? —You're right, believing is an absolutely horrible thing. And hope is a stupid trap. That's why I decided to act. This is war, young man! Tell me, which side are you on? —Which side, Toby?

Now Toby was mad. Aha! he exclaimed, the gentleman pretends he's neutral. He shows concern for peasant reality only in photographs! Interesting. Shameful, more than anything! I understand, then, when you say the little matter I'm occupied with now doesn't concern you. You're looking at the world through the lens of comfort and art. Cushy and isolated on your island. So your name is Robinson! I retorted that he was wrong, that in Berlin, I had slaved at gruelling little jobs to pay for my education, I'd had my share of hard times. —But at least, he went on, you can buy things. He closed his eyes again and said, very low, his hands moving in some strange ritual, What are you doing now,

Ruth? Nothing? So dream. To keep on dreaming takes energy, don't you think? Yes, you're right. Anyway, I'm working. Pray for me, for us. Don't be afraid, I'll get you out of there, my wonderful Ruth. . . . And while he was talking with his ghost, I closed my eyes and imagined myself in the cool of my Berlin apartment. Through thought I tried to flee from fire, from torture, from death.

MY LIFE IN BERLIN, the long, often dull days writing my articles upon returning from trips, the arguments, reconciliations, and outings with Oumi, like that time a few months ago. Oumi was hanging onto my arm, an orchestra set up in a corner of the huge salon was playing Bach, Minuet 1, Minuet 2, Minuet 3. A high society evening in a mansion on Torstraße, where an engagement was being celebrated. The glamourous union of Anja, Oumi's best friend, with a scrawny guy whose family had made a fortune in real estate. I didn't want to go, I had told my girlfriend, it wasn't my thing making conversation with characters from another century in a setting of plaster angels looking down from an immaculate vaulted ceiling, marble columns, grandiose Swarovski crystal chandeliers threatening to fall on your head, heavy velvet drapes with jacquard valances embroidered with gold thread. To find myself in that brightly lit salon wearing the suit of a man of the world while within me still echoed the words from those forgotten places, the starving world of Rajasthan and the Sahel, about which I had just written my umpteenth article. It's not out of disrespect, I said to Oumi, I just need a bit of time to make the transition between those republics of resourcefulness and eternal hope and our enviable life on the shores of the Rhine and the Thames. Time to go back across that nonexistent bridge between the muck and the glitter. . . . Oumi sulked for a week, so I finally gave in, and in recognition of the huge sacrifice I was making, she had promised me a memorable night.

Two days later, the evening came, with the velvet, the chandeliers, the gold, and everything else. The fiancée, on the arm of the one chosen by her fragile heart, was the personification of happiness, class, gaiety, her every gaze and gesture striving to support all the theories of love. We were three hundred carefully selected guests. How did they arrive at exactly three hundred? I had asked Oumi teasingly. Who was the unfortunate three-hundred-and-first one who wasn't chosen, who didn't get a passport to our shining world, the one who didn't have the right suit or the right dress for your dear friend's engagement?

In the middle of that room filled with dinner jackets, silk, tulle, and lace, there occurred a tragedy that shook the earth and the waters of the Spree. One of the waitresses moving through the forest of murmured refined courtesies, perfumed skin, and robotic smiles serving us champagne and petits fours, one of those unhappy anonymous creatures clothed in their insignificance, committed the sacrilege of allowing her tray of glasses of red wine to tip from her hand and fall upon the splendour and grace of the dress of one of the precious and ridiculous guests, who let out a shriek like a stuck beast. The shriek was followed by insults, Scatter-brain! Fool! Idiot! This isn't a gypsy camp! My dress! What will I do? —Am I wrong or did she rent her fur? I whispered in Oumi's ear as she took in the full extent of the catastrophe. The wave of our gaiety having frozen around the waitress and her victim, who was still spouting curses, I pinched Oumi's bare arm and said, Didn't I tell you all this careful vocabulary and gestures are a farce? . . . I watched our waitress, who maintained an enviable calm, staring at her victim, whose finery was drenched in the most expensive of Egon Müller-Scharzhof red wines.

Then the waitress exploded, Screw you, screw all of you with your ridiculous getups. Just because you're stuffed into that grotesque tube from an Italian couturier doesn't give you the right to talk to me like that! Do you have any idea what cotton, what blood and sweat went into making your rags? Screw you with your Claudie Pierlot, Eleven Paris, ba&sh, Comptoir des cotonniers, Maje, Sandro, Zadig & Voltaire, The Kooples, Armani, Burberry, Cerruti, Chanel, Valentino,

34

Versace, Roberto Cavalli, the hell with them all! . . . And our rebel, throwing the napkins she was clutching into the face of the persecuted guest, cut through the crowd and left the huge room in a beautiful finale of slammed doors. And Oumi whispered to me, If that girl can name all those brands and all those designers from memory, it's not because she hates them—unless she's writing a thesis on the subject. . . . I didn't reply, and the orchestra, which had kept playing during the five minutes when everyone stood frozen and the Earth stopped turning, carried on the Bach concert with brio, the music indifferent to our drama—or was it playing to cover up our hypocrisy?

IN THE EXHIBITION HALL, it wasn't the music but the heat that was unrelenting. I had hoped that the cool air would last a little longer under the assault of the heat wave—an hour, maybe two. I closed my eyes, trying to imagine myself under a more temperate sky. This climate seemed to have exiled me, I no longer belonged in this geography despite the fact that I was born in it, so I was fleeing with the remains of an obsolete history in my pockets. But Toby interrupted my flight, saying, Maybe it wouldn't be a bad idea to accept here and now that we're going to be hot. —I can't! I bleated. And there's no more air. I've visited hot countries! However, I had the advantage of being outside, often with a little wind. But tolerating this between four walls, no!

I was perishing on the floor, while the hands of my watch, unlike time between the walls of the room, continued moving. Toby went over to another print and removed it from the wall. He took his time opening the back of the frame and removing the photograph. He came back over to me and asked, What do you think of this one, Robinson? Am I wrong or is it not too bad? I couldn't deny it, the photograph was one of the ones I found successful, a harvest scene under a blue-grey sky, a young woman, her head wrapped in a multicoloured scarf, standing in the middle of a mound of cotton fibres that were almost blindingly white. She had grabbed a handful of cotton and thrown it over her head, and a young boy was leaping to try to catch the white balls, to snatch them from the wind and the birds. It was as if the two actors in the scene were engaged in a game whose rules they had mastered perfectly, a beautiful match in an incongruous setting and, besides the spontaneity and obvious truth of their movements, the shot—and there lay its success, in my view—accentuated the presence of that other, invisible, actor, the wind, which in the end reinforced the natural quality of the game. Another thing, the young woman and the boy were not displaying that horrible grimace, teeth bared, that was shown in most of the other photographs. Toby pursed his lips and said, No, you can't say it's ugly, this one. I could almost feel some sympathy for our photographer, but too bad, it's also going up in smoke. —Not that one, Toby! Choose one that's not worth anything! —Robinson, you're a stupid museum rat who doesn't act! No, sir, I'm not here to spare the organizers of this farce!

And with those words, Toby sprayed kerosene on a corner of the photograph and set it on fire with his lighter. And while I was twisting my wrists and ankles, trying unobtrusively to rid myself of my bonds—the damn fellow knew his knots!—Toby went over to the window and said, Hello, Commissioner, and the fire ate its way steadily through the glossy paper, helped along by a breeze. Ignoring my own misery, I felt a pang at seeing the photograph being reduced to ashes, the long, thin legs of the child who was leaping into the wind consumed, the frail arms of the woman obliterated, and I thought to myself that only the wind in the photograph would survive the carnage, unless the wind outside also devoured it.

Toby stood at the window for a few seconds and then came back to the middle of the room. He noticed my expression, which must have been one of disappointment. Don't tell me, he said, that this trivial little spectacle has made you sad? Nobody gives a damn about that photograph! You know, I don't remember seeing such a scene in our fields in recent months. I think the photographer was very good at setting up the shot. Or did he take that picture somewhere else, on some other planet where they celebrate in the cotton fields? I was right, Robinson, you're with them. . . . He drank from a gourd he had taken out of his pouch, caught his breath, and said, Well, Robinson, have a drink, we're only in chapter one of our troubles, drink before I put you on the pyre. And he shouted toward the outside, I couldn't be more serious, Mr Director, I must say my lighter works very well. So what's new? —We haven't just been standing here doing nothing, Ed shouted back. People have been contacted and they'll soon react. Shango chimed in, Think about what you're doing. And Toby responded, Oh, I know what I'm doing. I have my wits about me, gentlemen! But the trouble is, I don't know how long I'll be able to hold on to them.

38

I RECALLED OTHER TROUBLES, those of my grandfather in the mid-1980s, enraged, when he told us he no longer recognized or loved the landscape that lay before our eyes in the valley. It was true that, in the preceding months, frightful diggers, cultivators, and chainsaws had ravaged and razed a good part of the valley between the two peaks with misty summits. I wonder where the agoutis, the ground squirrels, the antelopes, and the valley monkeys could have fled to. Grandfather had said, Only the birds have some chance of escaping all this, and since the good Lord did not give us wings to fly far away, well, we're also done for! . . . The denuded plain had been covered with young oil palm plants, from the peak of Kebo in the south to that of Kpéta in the north. Grandfather had shouted, I have nothing but that now in front of my eyes, that boring, monotonous sea of green! Furious, he had put away his painting supplies or had left them in front of the house, I don't recall, and left, with his humble Bremen Mission pastor's Bible under his arm, to shut himself up until nightfall within the walls of his church, to pray, to search the pages of the book for that marvellous verse that would make the fields bloom again in another way. And while her husband was gone, Grandmother, tousling my hair with her energetic fingers, said, Your grandfather is annoyed, maybe he won't be able to work on his lovely paintings anymore. Where will he be able to get his inspiration now? From that bare landscape with no colour or warmth? I replied, But he could make us a painting of the valley of his dreams, couldn't he? The valley as he would have wanted it? Reinvent the trees and the grass and the birds that have fled to other lands.

Grandfather was not happy, the nature he wanted to paint was no longer recognizable, and as if that weren't enough, we had begun to observe new tree felling in the strip of wild land separating the plantation of palm trees from the horizon line. Grandfather rushed down to the village to speak with the chief, who, powerless or overwhelmed by everything, was taking comfort in palm wine and philosophy. The chief had told Grandfather that perhaps it wasn't a bad idea; a German company was building a cotton-ginning factory and an oil mill north of the palm plantation. You had to look on the bright side, the good peasants of the village would no longer have to spend their days pounding palm nuts in those hollow mortars dug into the ground as wide as craters. I remember that to console himself Grandfather had painted a scene in which ten splendid figures sweating and singing were pounding nuts and dancing, each with one foot raised on the red clay edge of the crater and the other foot on the grass and rocks. In the painting, the orange colour represented the pasty fibrous mass that formed under the pestles, which were made from long acacia branches. Grandmother said, The painting is beautiful, but it doesn't give you a sense of how the people's bodies are moving. Grandfather ignored the remark, already white with anger after his visit with the village chief, who had told him that it was his German fellow-citizens from the Ruhr who were building the plants, and concluded by saying, Our brothers from the West share the contract for our salvation—you, Pastor Hoffer, for the souls, and the builders of factories for the land. But what are you doing with the men themselves?

Years later, I would understand. Nothing was done with the men. The men were nothing, especially when they were Blacks. However, Samuel Brown's skin was not nothing, it was a land, and in 1884 at the Berlin Conference, it had been laid out on the desk of Otto von Bismarck, chancellor of Prussia, who outdid the overseer with his whip in the field in Alabama, the overseer who made bloody lines and furrows at random, while Bismarck, armed with a pen, divided the map and the man's back into territories for his friends in France, Belgium, England, etc. And red ink flowed on the skin. The land, under the whip and the quill. And Toby and the flame so close to my bare arm, and Ed outside repeating, You promise me, Toby, you won't touch your hostage! And Winnie knew that for a long time still, their skin would be subjected to torture, murder, or rape, because the great work had to continue.

37

DON'T TELL ME THAT, like any self-respecting Negro, you intend to spend your life loafing? That was the eternal question, said Toby, that Monsieur Antonin asked him at the end of the 1970s when he was approaching the age of fifteen. The master had said, Your father has told me you're doing well in school. You're an avid reader, which is still rare among these backward people. When we go to France, what you've learned in books will to some extent be useful for your duties as a major-domo. And as I've said, you seem much cleverer than most men here, who rarely think beyond their bellies and their cocks!

The master kept going on about it. Toby, I'll soon talk to your father about my desire to take you with me on the great day of my departure. I've been watching you and I no longer have any doubt, you're certainly a lot smarter than the asses around me. So you're coming with us to Aurillac. And if it happens that your intellectual abilities continue to surprise me, if your being a major-domo proves to be a waste, well, we'll assess the possibility that you pursue further studies. Then you'll be able to become, let's say, a lawyer, and produce fabulous arguments in defence of unfortunate souls and your people, whose problems are far from over. But in the meantime, shine these shoes for me. No one on this farm does it better than you. And Toby thought, Arguments in defence of bellies and cocks?

And anyway, Robinson, there's not much to defend anymore in our savannahs. The only thing left is a dilapidated house in the middle of the fields. It's imposing, nevertheless, a concrete structure, almost square, and still impressively solid, its off-white whitewash flaking in places, but more beautiful with time, blending into its surroundings of ochre earth, yellowed brush, and grey or brown tree trunks. The tiled roof is thick, too, and it supports a huge black plastic water tank. Like a strange hot-air balloon. If you should pass that way, you can climb onto a cinder block and look over the brick enclosure at the courtyard. You'll see the red-tiled patio in front with its four impressive columns painted blue, the patio where I spent long days checking my accounts. At the end of the gravel lane from the gate, wide stone stairs lead to the porch and the varnished mahogany door and four big windows with shutters of the same wood. It isn't really beautiful architecture, but it has the virtue of being solidly rooted in the ground. I recall the frightened poultry running in all directions outside. All around, on some twenty hectares, the abandoned fields are a disorderly carpet of seedlings, dead leaves, and dandelions. And perhaps, Robinson, Old Yambo's now empty little bags of earth are floating there, carried by the wind. And what was his idea in stuffing earth into bags for fear that it would disappear?

36

I WAS HOT, AND IT WAS IMPOSSIBLE to get rid of Toby or my shirt. I tried to dive into an imaginary lake. But the lapping of the water mingled with Grandmother's voice, saying, The heat, little one, reveals the truth of the body and the strength of a person's character. Don't run away from it! Your body is telling you that it's not yet ready to bear the hardships of life; your character, that it's fragile. You have only one choice, to endure and learn. . . . And now I had to endure Toby, who has taken two round metal bowls out of his bag, a very small one and a big one, painted yellow. I recognized them, when I lived in Le Port the women selling grain in the market used them to measure the quantities requested by customers. —These bowls belonged to Mara, Toby said. She and her husband lost everything after a disastrous season. They gave up their land to their creditors and ended up stuck on a tiny lot, a pen for animals, with empty eyes yellow with malaria. Mara then prostituted herself.

Toby continued, In the market in the largest town in the savannahs reigned the most corrupt merchants the heavens ever shat onto the earth. A moneylender who, when Mara and her family first went broke, had agreed to sell to them on credit the flour and oil they needed to survive. They had to feed their two kids, who by then were starving little animals watching with dead or envious eyes the joyous feasting of the birds in the baobabs above their heads. Mara had to find them something so they would stop hating the birds. But the loans had mounted, and our grocer lost patience, demanding immediate payment, in full. Payment, he repeated, undressing Mara with his eyes. The woman held out for a few days while the kids had nothing in their bellies but emptiness and noise. On day four, she gave in to the scoundrel, who, after enjoying her body, which was gaunt but still beautiful, gave her a bowl of millet. In the following days, it was the big bowl when he felt satisfied, the little one when he did not. This went on for many long weeks, unsuspected by the husband, whom Mara told that the despicable man was still giving them credit. Until the day the rumours in the market reached the husband's ears. And one sad evening, tears in his eyes, he slit Mara's throat; then he went to the market, where he tried to kill the merchant, who managed to run away and alert the cops. With Mara dead and their father in jail, the children were entrusted to dying grandparents.

Toby hung Mara's two bowls on nails. He said he would continue gathering things for his museum. He would ask the peasants if he could have certain unused tools or other objects that had been abandoned in the fields in return for a small sum. And in the back of a truck he'd bought he would pack an old scarecrow, a trowel whose metal had been eaten away by the rocky soil, a winnowing basket of palm fibre, items scattered at the foot of the buttes that in their former lives were parts of ploughs, a worn ploughshare, a twisted moldboard that must have turned over hectares of soil, a coulter that had left furrows in the valleys, Manga and Minumba hoes, a broken Rumpstad plough, an Arara combine in a thousand pieces that had been piled up against the trunk of a palm tree. Perhaps also, Robinson, I would find in the valleys some bags of earth forgotten there by old Corporal Yambo. He added that Yambo had finally croaked. From hunger and madness.

35

WHEN HE HAD PLACED THE BOWLS where he wanted them, Toby sat down again, this time against the wall on my left. He closed his eyes and opened them again right away, and read in my eyes the question, How did all this happen? I had to get out of this shitshow, but curiosity was pushing me against my will to dig a little deeper into Toby's life and his rotten luck. It was also my strategy, a very flimsy one, to get him to talk in order to gain time and banish visions of my execution. And he began to tell me more of his story. In 2010, when his old father had deserted him a mere few weeks after he had taken over the family farm, Toby had managed, with the advice of their two seasoned employees, to keep going. Considering the preceding seasons, it was practically a miracle. The cotton had grown that year, although he had to increase the amount of organic manure and urea-based nitrogen fertilizer added to the soil. It was beautiful cotton, he recalled, long, impeccably white silky fibres. He had no trouble selling the year's harvest to the cotton companies, twenty-five tonnes of it, which had required the hiring of temporary employees. Toby remembered it as a promising beginning and felt he had been right to leave his job as a librarian. The second year had not been as good because less rain had fallen, but they managed twenty tonnes.

Things had begun to go downhill in the cursed year 2012, when caterpillars, creatures of the devil, invaded the fields, followed by white flies that were equally devastating, reducing all their efforts to nothing. They sprayed the fields with the pesticides recommended by the National Cotton Company, to no avail. The company agreed to reduce the debt the peasants had incurred, but, Toby said, Having ended up with a harvest of two meagre tonnes, which was not even enough to pay my employees, I couldn't pay back my other loans. He said the dream was dead, and all he could do was run away from the fields and never come back. The angry land was pushing the peasants to the edges of the cities and the filthy, depraved back streets, turning them into rats scrounging scraps amid the rubbish in public dumps. Returning to the city periodically during those dark times, he drowned his sorrows in drink in the shadows of a hotel room in an alley of the old quarter. The girls and the Friday night partying no longer existed, those carefree Fridays had disappeared from his calendar.

He was about to throw himself into the abyss when he caught hold of a hand held out to him by the devil in a suit and tie. The year 2012 was coming to an end. The devil, elegant, well-dressed, and polite, introduced himself as Zak Bolton, ambassador of The Firm, saying, Ambassador is a very grand title, I'm just a simple broker for the gods of cotton. Have you heard of The Firm? . . . Yes, Toby had read a few articles about The Firm, some highly complimentary, some very critical. —Which had made me suspicious, he said. Bolton asked him if he would like to talk about Bt cotton with him, and added, I must say, given the state of your fields, it wouldn't be a bad idea. They made an appointment for the following week. Toby was very sceptical the next time he met with that strange fellow, who immediately offered him his first GMO seeds, the herbicides, and his valuable expertise at an attractive price. Zak Bolton must have been very persuasive, or else his mere presence, his magnetic aura swept away any capacity to resist. I'll give it a try, Toby finally said, with some hesitation. At the point where I am now. . . . His bank gave him a loan to launch the new venture. The Firm's name had an influence on its decision, a substantial one. Hadn't The Firm, with the backing of the Minister of Agriculture, promised the growers five tonnes of cotton per hectare when they were barely managing to produce one using the good old-fashioned methods?

There was no miracle. With the new products provided by The Firm, Toby was able to fend off the pests, but only for one season. However, his harvest was far from his expectations, a little less than ten tonnes. The reason was simple, the fibre of the new Bt cotton was shorter, less heavy, also less white. Toby sighed, If in that goddamn year 2013 I could at least have gotten my price for those ten miserable tonnes of poor-quality cotton! But no, the buyers said take it or leave it! . . . In short, Toby had to sell his poor made-in-America Bt cotton for a crust of maize bread. And, surprise, the next season, a new kind of pest had made its appearance in the fields, and the two sprayings of pesticides that, according to The Firm, were supposed to curb them proved ineffective. Toby continued, On the farm, Robinson, I was working with my two employees and some fifteen seasonal workers. We stepped up the use of those damn products—in vain! We were in deep shit. That shit, Robinson, is their Bollgard II, their goddamn seeds. They fast-tracked production in their bloody laboratories. They were in a huge rush, and according to what I read, they did only two crosses of biological elements to obtain their seeds. A backcross, they call it. And, listen, normally it takes six crosses of a hybrid gene with a parent, I mean a more stable seed. So, just like in a horror movie, they created a monster cotton like nothing that existed before! And to further crush the peasants, treacherous agents working for both The Firm and the Ministry of Agriculture accused them of botching the growing of the Bt cotton. For example, they claimed the peasants didn't spray the products properly, or simply didn't spray at all. Lies! Those people were cowards who refused to accept responsibility! That's how we got to this point, Robinson. And I promise them fire in this lovely little museum. Did I tell you that they showed us something else in America? There in Georgia, they showed us the dream. Yes, I went to Georgia, in August 2013, while my first GMO cotton plants were growing. There in Georgia was the rotten dream, the old oaks in the squares, and Ruth.

34

SURROUNDED BY THE ARTWORKS of that joker Jean Lenoir, I thought back to the work Grandfather adored so much that it was almost unhealthy. In my mind I watched the movie of the first time I went to see that work, in Vienna in that ugly autumn of dark skies in 1998, three months after I arrived in Berlin to attend university. I barely glanced at the shrubbery shaped into balls and cones in front of the Italian Renaissance building, nor did I stop to admire the impressive gilded dome with its blue stained glass windows. I headed straight to it. And when I saw it, I felt very strange and quite alone, it was like a huge window offering you the spectacle of another world, a window through which you could escape. And that was what I did. I didn't go into that scene of another time, but elsewhere, because a horrible knot had formed in my stomach. I dashed off to the other rooms and planted myself in front of other pieces, magnificent works, a sad crucifixion scene signed Rogier van der Weyden, a little blue hippopotamus from ancient Egypt with a plump body covered in triangular patterns, a mosaic of Theseus defeating the Minotaur. I wandered for a good hour before coming back to stand in front of the painting, and I understood why my stomach was in knots; it was the feeling of having completely missed everything Grandfather had told me in our talks about the painting, the people in their revelry, the roofs of brownish thatch, and the grey sky in the background with a glow above what could be a church. I hadn't seen that, to Grandfather, the momentary lightness of the peasant dance was a refuge from the harshness of life.

On that first visit to the museum, I was taken back to my own history, that of a child raised by people who wanted to teach him to be honest and real and to grasp the rare truth of a hand held out to support him in the midst of tragedy—life, essentially a tragedy?—or invite him to celebrate for a moment, to forget, to resist depression, in that peasant dance, with the bagpipe player and his red-faced companion who holds out a pitcher to him. And again Toby held the lighter near my arm. Back off! I shouted, and Ed, panicky, yelled, Don't start that again, Toby! —So what news do you have for me? Toby asked. Things aren't moving! —Toby, government ministers have been informed of your action, replied Shango, and I've just been notified that a special mission will be dispatched to the savannahs to listen to the peasants' grievances and provide the best solution. —Could you be lying, Commissioner? asked Toby. And what grievances, anyway? We want the two hundred million, period! —You're not being reasonable, Toby, Shango said. The government and the museum have worked hard on the exhibition, and you're going to screw everything up! —I don't care! Toby retorted. And you're going to lose a man tied up on the floor!

33

2:25, MY WATCH READ, AND I WAS LOST. Toby stood up again. He went over to his bag and took out a package with an elastic around it. He went back to his place and opened the kraft paper wrapping, releasing cement dust, and I could see that there were photos inside. My exhibition, he said, I believe in it. He sighed, looking at the first shots. I was curious, and also determined to keep talking with him so as to give Shango and Ed time to act. Can I see them, Toby? I asked. From where he was sitting, he showed me the first photo, and I jerked backward, forgetting that behind me there was only a cold, hard wall, the wall for the condemned man's execution. The photo was of a hanged man. A man suspended by his neck from a bough of a tree in front of a shack, watched over by the wind and the birds. The clothes of the unfortunate man were worn, his tattered pants barely covering his scrawny legs. His head was turned slightly to one side, as if to answer a last call from an angel or the devil on his shoulder. Toby sighed and said, We lost Wali a couple of weeks ago. He did himself in. He was flat broke. And look at this one, I found it in his things. It was taken not long ago, Wali was smiling and joking with people in the market. And this one here. . . . It was a picture of a stream whose water was a suspicious colour, with a completely white lamb dipping its pink muzzle in the water. The stream, Toby said, ran through the land of another grower who took a chance on Bt cotton. He showed me ten more pictures of sad farmers and dead landscapes. Then, smiling, he walked over to the photographs in the exhibition. And ten snapshots were added to the "Peasant Dance" series, thumbtacked in the space that had been occupied by the two photographs Toby had burned. He went back to his bag and pulled out a piece of rope about a metre long. He said gravely, You can guess, can't you, Robinson? It's a piece of the rope Wali used to hang himself. Toby made a slipknot in the rope and hung it on another nail. He had prepared things well. —So, he asked, what do you think of my effort? —What effort, Toby? You're at a dead end, and your miserable photos from old family albums won't change anything! Plus you're wasting everyone's time! I repeat, you won't gain anything alone, nothing! And besides, what will you do with the two hundred million? Pay off your debts? And after that? What's your follow-up plan? —So you're a pessimist, Robinson? —Don't call me that, Toby! —Why shouldn't I? I think it suits you, you're a solitary character, it fits you perfectly. —I won't answer that. —I have to put captions on my works. You see, I'm totally serious. I'm taking action! Can you loan me your notepad? —This travesty will get you nowhere.

Without waiting for my permission, Toby came over and grabbed the notebook and pen lying on the floor against my thigh, beside my camera. He returned to his place against the wall and for five minutes he was hard at work. When that laborious task was finished, he handed me the first rectangle of paper, on which I read "Savannahs of the North, 2014, the Lamb and the Yellow River"; another one, describing a photo of a peasant with empty eyes sitting in front of his hut, his impotent hands open in his lap, "Toula at the End"; a third, "Wali Hanged by Bt Cotton"; a fourth, summing up, a photo of the angry growers carrying placards, protesting in front of the offices of the Cotton Company of La Savane, "Peasant Anger"; another, accompanying an image of peasants at work, "Serfs." —Very inspired words, I said, trying to get a rise out of him. —I won't refuse the compliment, Robinson, he smiled. —But they're too lyrical. —Do you think so? —Yes, for sure. —What do you have against lyricism? —Nothing, but here you should be more restrained, more direct. —Oh, I see, I see. But "Serfs," that's restrained. We cotton growers *are* serfs, Robinson. I remember reading an article in which a peasant from Burkina Faso was compared to a serf. —You don't think it's a bit exaggerated, Toby? —No. We toil like donkeys for the real lords of cotton: The Firm, which makes the goddamn seeds, and the market, which pays abysmal prices for our harvest. But, to come back to your remark, my little phrases are not bad even though they may seem like they came straight out of a poetry book. —I have some doubts about their effectiveness, Toby. —Too bad! I'm going to go put them under my prized photos.

He went to put the words up, holding the pages from the notebook as if they were something of great value, a rare substance, pearls or gold dust, pure and wild, as rare as the animal skin of Samuel Brown, and the whip tore it open, red, in thousands of posts and ports, Cape Coast, Gorée, Zanzibar, and Samuel was a tree, a hevea that had been bled, from which rubber flowed, Samuel was precious rubber, so why then kill him because he no longer had the strength to gather the cotton? It's stupid! Grandmother would have said, it seems that the one who holds the whip doesn't think further than his primal, brutal hate. Yes, little one, it's really a stupid thing to do. . . . But Grandmother would have been wrong. Unlike Winnie, who no longer had any doubt: the whip and the rage had to continue to play their role in the great work. And for the work to be perpetuated, actions like those of the overseer of Alabama had to be repeated, intensified, refined.

ACTIONS . . . I REMEMBERED the care Grandfather took with his paintings, how laboriously he drew on the canvas the peasants' actions and
facial expressions over the course of the seasons, their outstretched
arms moving theatrically, hoeing, weeding, and pruning, machetes in
their fists. The care he took drawing the thin legs and the arms digging
in the earth at seeding time, the angles of the bent torsos and stiff-
ened limbs, the spare, straight silhouette of the man beating a tam-tam
hanging from a worn rope around his neck to spur the workers on, the
bare arms of the women with scarves tied around their heads holding
out heaven-sent gourds of palm wine to the sweaty bodies of the men.
The care he took depicting the harvest scenes in colour and line, the
arms balancing baskets of ears of millet, maize, or sorghum on burned
heads, the actions of those arms opened to pick, gather, lift, and load
all those things, actions and lives that an old pastor who loved painting and Bruegel the Elder nearly as much as God tried to immortalize
in his way. To paint the dance, the same eternal, sublime peasant cho-
reography of celebration in the peaceful, simple, beauty of meadows
immutable in their majesty, while, with the changing times, the peasants of former days dead and forgotten, it seemed that the portraits
that would be made of the new tenant farmers would be different, cold
depictions of the pain and the disaster when there was no longer anything to hope for from the dead land, when the beauty of the spontane-
ous actions would be replaced for good by the programmed circus of
the machines, announcing the end of the dances out in the fields, yet,

and I knew this from wandering in the fields behind my grandparents' house as a child, that past embellished by the hands of a painter also had its harshness and miseries, with its gloomy, rainless sky, cracked earth, swarms of ferocious locusts devouring the plants, days of fear and anxiety, eyes staring at the empty granaries. Perhaps the present is not so harsh, said Grandfather, and there were afternoons when he was able to look up from the pattern emerging under his brush and say to me, Come, let's leave behind these things that express nothing but selfish obsessions and fears of mine for a while. It could be that things are not so bad on these plateaus, my parishioners, growers since before their migration from the Egypt of the pharaohs, tell me they're happy. They even give a little more to the Sunday collection because, they proclaim, Christ has listened to their prayers and eased their toil. With the oil mill operating at full capacity, they're no longer forced to pound palm nuts for long afternoons, but, believe me, the oil produced by the factory is not the best, it has a horrible smell of engines and rot! It seems that the workers, who have to work very fast, mess up the cleaning of the tubs into which the oil flows, part of which goes to the soap factory that has been built in the valley below the Plateau de Daye. Their soap is full of lye and it burns your skin. But maybe that's the way things have to be? Is that progress? I doubt it, my lad.

31

2:35 PM. I WAS SUFFOCATING. Thinking of my early life, of a morning sky in the cool air, on a trail with Grandmother holding my hand, while Toby continued his feline prowl in search of prey. His hands shoved into his pockets full of holes, he let his eyes wander aimlessly over the ceiling with its white dots, then came back and stood in front of me, his piercing eyes staring into mine. Tell me, he said. —Tell you what? —Why did you come and hang out in this gallery? If, as you say, you write articles on poor people and their problems, shouldn't you be far away, in some hole forgotten by the world? —I don't spend my whole life in the hellholes of the world, Toby. —You prefer to just dip your toe in them, right? —That's not what I said. —Then why did you come and gawk at these miserable photos? —Don't people have the right to be curious? —You could have shown up at the vernissage like everybody else. —I wanted to be alone with the photographs to try to discover the meaning, the true meaning, of the exhibition. Some people go to museums for pleasure. For me, it's that and also something more, a search, a quest. —I see. You search, but you don't do anything. You took lots of notes and pictures. —I've already written a few articles on the peasants and GMOs, which explains why my friend Ed Kaba, who runs this institution, thought the event might interest me. —What newspapers or magazines are you published in? —*Afriterre, Geopolis, Terra Nostra.* —I see. But sometimes it takes starting a fire to shake up these crooks who manipulate us ridiculous puppets. So, you go looking for trouble, you listen, you observe, and you write articles. Are you at least well paid for it? —Well enough. I've been doing it for ten years. My last investigation was of peasant suicides in India. —Good timing! As you've seen clearly, it's not the rope but the debt that tightens around your throat in the end, right? You know, my friend Wali, three days before he hanged himself, he came to see me. He wanted a very small loan. Just to keep going, he said. I didn't have anything. Shit! If I'd been able to give him even a measly ten-thousand-franc note, maybe he wouldn't have done it. —You can't know that, Toby. —Maybe he could have held on another day, and then, the next day, by some miracle, a kind soul could have come to save him? —What kind soul? I don't see any around here. —Fair enough. So your goal then would be to produce an article on us growers on our unpredictable savannahs? —I don't know. I wanted to see first. —Don't waste your time writing an article. Can't you make movies?

He said he still believed in cinema. A good movie, where you simply needed to let the actors move, speak, fight, and the truth would emerge through their movements. A great cinematic work on the peasants of the South, Toby said, and if we want the whole world to see that movie, well, Robinson, it has to be American! The huge Hollywood machine has to come and film here in our savannahs. —And who's going to produce that great movie, Toby? Nobody is interested in you. —They've made plenty of movies with slaves toiling like beasts in the plantations of Virginia or Georgia. Stuff to make you bawl. So they could very well set the same thing here! —Would you demand pity from the rest of the world? —I don't give a damn about people's pity! I'm talking about collaboration, Robinson. They should come and film something pure, something true, the complete opposite of their ridiculous, artificial melodramas on movie sets in California! Imagine the magnificent, powerful movie they could make with our misery, as common as it is! —Even if someone financed your film, it's far from certain that people would rush to the theatres to watch it. —Why not? —Are you playing dumb, Toby? It suits you. Nobody is interested in you. —But if we had a good cast to portray our story in the fields of GMOs . . .

57

He presented a list of famous actors, illustrious American Blacks who were successful on the stages of Broadway and the sets of Los Angeles. He told me he could easily see Danny Glover playing him. I complimented him on his modesty. And then, he said, Denzel Washington, Will Smith, Don Cheadle could play tenant farmers, wearing worn, tattered clothes and carrying heavy bales of cotton with the sun beating down on their faces. —You're forgetting the girls, Toby. —What girls? —The actresses. You'll need actresses too. Without them your movie won't get much interest. It isn't only guys who toil in the fields. —I wasn't finished, Robinson. Personally, I really like Viola Davis. Do you think she'd agree?

30

TOBY TOOK ANOTHER BLACK-AND-WHITE PRINT down from the wall. It showed the same rural landscape occupied by peasants smiling broadly. He curled his lip. Hmm, Robinson, he said, it's written beside the frame that this is a loan from an institution called The Foundation. I remember hearing about it. Philanthropists, that's how the people who set up this suspicious thing present themselves. But we know they blindly support The Firm. Well, their lovely work is also going to go up in smoke. . . . And he went over to the window again, where he subjected the photograph to the same treatment as the previous ones.

From the street came Commissioner Shango's voice again, hoarse from tobacco, saying, You obviously don't want to cooperate, Toby! Are you still hoping to come out of this as an honest, law-abiding citizen? —We'll see, Shango. And you'd better get going on fixing the goddamn air conditioning! . . . On the radio Toby had turned on, a journalist said he had just arrived at the scene of the hostage taking, I'm standing in front of the Museum of the Green Revolution, which was supposed to be officially opened tonight. An individual by the name of Toby Kunta has been holed up for almost three hours in the main exhibition room. He was hired a few weeks ago as a guard. The Museum, concerned about security, had provided the guard with the necessary surveillance and self-defence tools, including a Taser, which he used at the stroke of noon to neutralize the individual he has taken hostage. The hostage is a freelance journalist who was planning to write an article on the event that was to take place this evening.

Toby turned to me and said, So you came here to write a nice article on this masquerade. I wasn't wrong, you're on their side! —My friend Ed Kaba had to justify my presence in the hall before the opening of the exhibition. I'm not on anyone's side! —So that's your approach? Never stick your neck out. You didn't give a damn about me. —Whatever you say, Toby. Anyway, nothing would have kept me from writing about this exhibition! . . . My anger had returned; I was mad at Toby for making me a dead man walking.

Toby just sighed and continued his conversation with his ghost. Siesta time is over, Ruth. I know you no longer take your nap with your face turned up toward where the woodcocks perch. But I can't help imagining you lying under an oak tree, your straw hat over your eyes and your arms cushioning your neck. You've taken your boots off and you curl your toes and make them crack with a sound that attracts the attention of a squirrel a metre away struggling with a nut as hard as a pebble from the Coosa River that flows through your village. Are you really asleep, with your head against the root of the oak tree? And what colour are the fields? . . . What help will your skin be to me in my battle, Robinson? Yes, burn it, to shake up those people loitering outside. . . . The little flame came near my skin again, so near that it seemed I could feel it nipping at me. —No! I shouted. —This is taking too long, gentlemen! barked Toby. What's the news from The Firm? —Discussions are under way with them, replied Shango. —So hurry it up! —Make a gesture, Toby, free your hostage! urged Ed Kaba. —What hostage? I only see a bundle of sticks I'm about to set on fire in the middle of the fields. . . . In Alabama, Winnie thought at night of stealing all the whips and all the violence of the overseer James Hoogan and burning them. But she was not stupid, she knew that the entire great work would have to be burned, in a ceremony filled with cries of victory in the middle of the fields.

THE FIELDS. THERE WAS A TIME when Grandfather stopped being interested in landscapes, his brush moving away from the forms of plains, peaks, and rivers to those of men. He said, After all, what is most important in the works of Bruegel is the people, isn't it? Those peasants in drab short tunics of lambswool, with hastily made poulaines on their feet, those people my master immortalized in paintings such as *The Harvesters, The Return of the Herd*, and *The Peasant Wedding*. That was how Grandfather spoke, his eyes shining, delighted with the first paintings in the new series he had started, on people working the land on our plateaus, dressed in clothes worn threadbare. The men often wore shirts full of holes, wrinkled, dark with mud and sweat, their long sleeves ripped by tree branches or half torn out from wear over seasons of labour, and baggy pants of rough cotton made by the village weaver, tied around the waist with cord or vines, and on their feet the inevitable crude sandals made from old tires. The women wore longer dresses in fabric printed in various patterns but just as washed out, dresses or wrappers that were very wide for ease of movement, and Grandfather had accentuated the way the garments flared, which made Grandmother ask, Hans, what wind is lifting the fabric of those dresses? Or are those women twirling for the pleasure of embracing the wind? Or are they dancing? And supposing that they're dancing, what in the painting suggests that this is a moment of joy amid the ears of grain and the baskets scattered in the field? . . . Grandfather smiled, Let's say that for the women it's always a celebration. There's a lightness, a carefreeness, a pure joy in them. —Are you joking? retorted Grandmother. They work themselves to death in those fields, not to mention the brats that wear them out and the husbands who drain them of their last bit of strength in the night. —You're getting on my nerves, Fania! replied the artist, not unhappy at having perhaps produced a good painting, his peasant dance, the peasants lost in a forgotten countryside of Africa, his brush having refrained from overly embellishing the image, the attire, or the dust-covered faces.

That's how my grandfather lived, until that morning in January 1996 when he stopped painting. I had returned for the weekend from the capital, where I was studying at the *lycée*. The aging pastor's spare silhouette was in front of his easel, which he had set up outside the house, as was his habit. In front of his eyes, the same landscape, the oil mill—which was then operating at reduced capacity for an unknown reason—the plantation of palm trees, the peaks of Kpéta and Kebo facing each other as they had for millennia. Out of the corner of my eye, I observed him standing motionless in front of that nature he had discovered a half-century earlier, those plateaus to which he belonged, because he had long ago stopped considering the possibility of a return to the shores of the Weser. A new pastor appointed by the Presbyterian Church of the country had taken over three years earlier, which had given him lots of time to try to paint his great work, the ultimate oil that would fix for eternity what remained of joy and lightheartedness in the fields of our part of the tropics. He would get up at dawn and try repeatedly to create the essential painting, his brush in his long fingers, exhausting himself. However, watching powerless, we saw that he was discouraged by what he was producing, scenes he found trite and without style. He tried until that morning when, after standing in front of the canvas without being able to make a single brushstroke, he stowed his equipment, never again to take it out, despite the encouragement of Grandmother, who could clearly see that he was dying.

IT WAS LESS MUGGY, MY EXHAUSTED BODY was telling me, but perhaps that was an illusion. On the trail in the cool mornings, Grandmother would always hold my hand, and now Toby, in our prison, went to get some display stands lying against the wall beside one of the emergency exits. He unfolded five of them, very tall little metal shelves. Then he went back to his bag and took out some strange items. There were two pieces of cardboard. On the first one he had pasted a handful of cotton. On the second one there another handful. He walked over to my corner and asked, Do you see the difference between these two products? You'll observe the remarkable whiteness of this one, and the length of the fibre. Now look at the other one. It's not the same, is it? It's like a washed-out gray, and the fibre is as short as the hairs on my chin. In the exhibition I'm setting up, Robinson, I am showing these samples. . . . And he went and placed them on the display stands. Then he held out a bottle filled with a white liquid and asked, Can you guess what this is? Milk, amigo. Bad milk, deadly! . . . On the bottle, he had stuck a danger label, a skull and crossbones. That bottle also took its place on a display stand. Another bottle followed, which contained some murky yellowish water. He continued, I told you about one of our waterways whose colour we can no longer recognize, right? Well, here's a nice sample. . . . The fourth exhibit he showed me was a photograph, a print in standard A4 format, in which a dozen sheep were lying on their sides in the middle of a field. —You will notice that those poor creatures have huge bellies. And that there's a brownish drool running from their dead open mouths. . . . He then showed me another piece of cardboard, on which there were leaves of cotton that had been dried. He put it on a display stand and came back to his place against the wall.

He asked, Did we have to sacrifice our beautiful cotton for that ugly, shrivelled stuff The Firm palmed off on us? He spoke of a certain Alpha Bello, who had always been a herder and who was also ruined. —And if he had only been ruined, Robinson! Alpha's kids suffered from a strange ailment, they puked up their guts and all the waters of their entrails. Alpha thinks it's because of the cows' milk the kids were drinking. And only a tenth of his cows are left, three half-dead heifers out of a herd of thirty. My friend Alpha has been raising animals for a quarter-century, and he's never seen anything like it! And I must add that his land is next to mine and the poor cows have always eaten cotton leaves along with other forage. In recent months Alpha no longer recognizes his animals. Epidemics happen sometimes, it's the law of nature, but never to this extent. Tell me, what do you really think of The Firm? —It has wreaked havoc and desolation here and elsewhere. —Are you serious or are you putting me on again? Because if you keep trying to make a fool of me, you'll be the next work I burn. —I'm a work of art? Thank you for the compliment, Toby. —I didn't say a good work of art. —Thank you. — Ah! I almost forgot, Toby said, picking up his pieces of paper again. I'm listening to you, Robinson. Your help in captioning my precious new samples will be invaluable. If you cooperate, maybe I won't burn you. Let's do the first one, the good and the bad cotton. What would you say?

This ritual seemed to be making me forget my stressful situation. And while Toby was writing, I would continue my surreptitious manoeuvres to rid myself of the solid sailor's ropes that were constricting my joints. I said, Toby, if I cooperate you won't come near me again. —You're not in a position to make any demands, Robinson. I'm listening to you. So? —For the first one, we can put "Traditional cotton with long white fibres, thick and silky." For the other one, "Bt cotton, less white, light, with very short fibres." Toby laughed, You didn't search very far for your vocabulary. —That's how you annotate items displayed in a museum. Once again, you aren't writing poetry here. —Why not? The visitors would be more sensitive to what they see if we made a little effort with the words, don't you think? But let's continue. And the bottle of devil's milk? —"Cow's milk that was probably poisoned, because the animals fed on forage from plants that were genetically modified and treated with pesticides." —Probably, you say? You're refusing to see the obvious, Robinson! I won't keep the adverb. And the bottle of murky water? —What's the name of the stream, Toby? —Akama. —Then write "Water from the Akama stream polluted by chemical spills in the cotton fields." —Ah! Could you be starting to take me seriously? —Let's say I'm giving you the benefit of the doubt. —I don't need your generosity, Robinson. And for the photo of the dead sheep? —Put "Livestock that are dying en masse after consuming genetically modified leaves." —Do you believe that or are you putting me on? —What do you think? —I don't know. But let's get on with it. —I'm exhausted, Toby. Figure it out for yourself. —So, for the last sample, I'll write "Goddamn Bt cotton leaves!" —That's unprofessional. —I don't give a damn! At least it's more convincing than those phony dances or that ridiculous twitching displayed around us!

TOBY, I SAID, OTHER CHARACTERS LEAP and twirl around in that dance, which has been going on for five centuries and a few seasons. I recalled the question Oumi, my ex, a tormented kid, asked me the time we went to see the painting in Vienna. Another time, perhaps the tenth, because after my first visit to the Kunsthistorisches Museum there were others, a score at least, yes, I would go to the Ringstraße once or twice a year, whenever I could, to see it, or rather see them, in what was now a regular rendezvous, staying there for hours under the mournful gaze of the guard, who was eager to finish his shift, standing motionless there because, quite simply, I could not be elsewhere; from the first time, those people carousing spoke to me, saying they had something to confess, a secret to share with me, the secret that Grandfather had wanted me to discover for myself. So, Oumi's question, then, was, What is the meaning of this village carnival? What are those people celebrating? A baptism, a wedding, a religious rite? The painter doesn't provide any clues about that. Surprising, isn't it? ... . And after that Oumi kissed me passionately despite the crowd of visitors around us, like the lovebirds wearing caps on the left side of the painting, a very comical gesture, and she added, If they don't bother to take off their strange headgear, it must not be a carnival day, so then I ask you again, What is the meaning of this circus?

What do the smiling, resigned, or worried faces of these peasants mean? That was the question that gnawed at me, that induced me, after Vienna, to scour other museums looking for what was supposed to be my truth. And that day in Amsterdam at the Van Gogh Museum, when I found myself in front of *The Potato Eaters*, I'd thought I'd grasped it. At first, that same gesture, the habit of not keeping everything for yourself, as in *The Peasant Dance* when the revellers pass around full pitchers or offer a drink to their neighbours. The same ritual in the Van Gogh, in the action of the peasant in the middle of the painting offering the woman sitting on his left the valued tuber. However, the most striking thing in the scene is the lamp hanging over the heads of the calm, stoic eaters. A faint, weak light that hardly reveals them to our eyes, to the world. And I said to myself, if we can make out the faces of those people, it might be less thanks to the lamp than to the artist who immortalized them. Poor people brought out of the shadows by the painter. For them, light had to be created. Was that what Grandfather, too, had tried to do? To bring out of the shadows the coarse country folk of our plateaus, to show what there was of carefreeness and lightness in them, qualities not immediately discernible in their closed, impassive faces, like those of Van Gogh's potato eaters or of Samuel Brown taken from the darkness of night, from the dawn of time on a morning in 1850 in a cotton field in Alabama through the whip and death, the overseer James Hoogan marking a territory as dead as his sad heart, Toby coming back to my arm with his lighter. Stop! I shouted at him. And Ed Kaba, angry, called to him, Toby, discussions are under way, we'll come back to you soon with news, so stop mistreating your hostage, let him go! And don't destroy the works in the exhibition, which could still go ahead if you come to your senses. It has cost a lot to organize all this. And Shango said, Listen to us. Make a gesture. —It's simple, Commissioner, Toby said, I want our two hundred million in the account whose number I gave you! Who do you think you're toying with? Maybe the smell of burned flesh would shake you up?

26

THE REPORTER OTI SALAM CAME BACK on the air. The sporadic screams of the hostage lead us to think that his kidnapper is subjecting him to some horrible torture, he said. So, are our authorities going to hurry up and comply with his demands? Toby guffawed, They're worried about you, Robinson. Do you feel less alone with this bit of attention? —I'll feel better outside these walls. —And what about me? I'd give anything right now to be on the Makina Loka dance floor. No, I'm kidding. I have no regrets. —But is there someone waiting for you outside that you'd like to see after all this? —Affirmative. —Ruth? —You could say that. And you, Robinson, if you died here now, would someone come and weep over your remains? —No. —No parents? A lover? —No. —You really *are* Robinson Crusoe. And to tell the truth, although I still think calling this exhibition "The Peasant Dance" is nothing but a way for our authorities to continue to sneer at the growers, I for one am almost inclined to think Bruegel was right. In our cotton fields, we have nothing anymore now, but we hold each other close. And we move because we have to do something with our bodies. —I see. You want to die united, as one. That way, you make it easy for the Grim Reaper. He won't need to cut you down one by one. —You're pissing me off! Death is already in us. But you're in danger of dying alone, Robinson. —What difference would it make? But would you tell me how you planned all this, Toby?

A siren sounded in the distance in the overheated city, and Toby told me that a month ago, with little to be done in his fields anymore—he'd had to lay off his two employees—he had hung around the capital for three days, getting drunk in the clandestine saloons and bars along his way, until he got to the outskirts of the city, to a vacant lot with a huge crater in the laterite where the fine citizens would dump their garbage. He said, My eyes were blurry and my head foggy, and I'd decided to end it all. You won't believe me, Robinson, but I had taken a few steps towards the edge of the abyss when I was stopped short by a voice behind me that I immediately recognized. The voice of an angel or the devil, as the case may be, Zak Bolton, the guy from The Firm, saying, You wouldn't do that, would you, Toby? What would Ruth think? . . . I stood frozen at the edge of the abyss, and when I turned around, my eyes still blurry, I saw the guy, dressed to the nines, gray suit, felt hat pulled down over his forehead, his face hidden by the smoke rising from the cigarette in his fingers. The guy continued, You wouldn't do that to Ruth, would you? You're stronger than all the gods, Toby, because, somewhere, there's a woman who loves you. —Who are you? I finally reacted, rubbing my eyes to distinguish the form facing me. The man laughed, a throaty laugh, and by the time I was able to make out the scene in front of me, he had disappeared.

Toby had rushed back to the heart of the city and sat down on the single bench in a garden in ruins, his head in his hands. Someone selling newspapers had come and pestered him, and he had bought one, mainly to get rid of the guy. And leafing through the paper, he had come across this ad on the Help Wanted page: *The Museum of the Green Revolution is looking for a security guard. No special skills required. Must be in good physical condition and willing to work nights. Call 90 90 90 91 for an interview.* What was this Museum of the Green Revolution all about? Was it a sign from the smoking angel who had come and stopped him from committing suicide? . . . That was how, the next day, Toby found himself face to face with my friend Ed Kaba, the newly appointed director of the Museum of the Green Revolution. Toby had said to himself, A security guard, why not? He was stressed, not by the interview but because all night long he had tried in vain to call Ruth, whose telephone was turned off. And before Ed asked him the first question, Toby declared he was an insomniac who killed time during the night by reading or staring at the stars to determine which one was going to fall on us. Ed had a good laugh and replied, So the Apocalypse is imminent? —Affirmative, boss. And contrary to what optimistic or stupid country people believe, everyone is going to go! . . . And by the end of that conversation, Toby had been hired by my friend Ed.

My tormentor went over the two weeks preceding his action. He said that as soon as he took up his position he was informed by Ed of the preparations for the exhibition. The title "The Peasant Dance" had made him laugh bitterly. He was eager to see what it was going to look like, but when someone called to tell him his friend Wali had hanged himself, he decided to take action. He was finishing his night shift, it was dawn. As Toby said poetically, At the break of dawn, my friend Wali hanged himself amid the cotton fields. —But you told me it was in front of his hut, Toby! —What difference does it make, Robinson? Let's just say this is my eulogy for Wali. —You're inspired. —In slave-owning America, they would hang Blacks from the trees, high and short. Today, The Firm is still doing the job. —You're exaggerating. —You're being stubborn, Robinson! Toby retorted. He said that after the phone call informing him of Wali's death, he had rushed back to the savannahs. The idea for what he called his counter-exhibition only came to him later. He thought of Ruth, who was still not answering his phone calls or his questions on Messenger. Ruth, who also collected things.

On the floor, exhausted, I tried to stretch. Looking him in the eye, I said, If you set fire to this building, no one will see the things in your exhibition. You went to a lot of trouble. It would spoil everything. —I know that very well. And supposing they kill me before I have time to light my fire, they'll throw these things right in the garbage. And you will have been the sole visitor to my museum.

MEMORY CAME AND LIFTED ME on its crazy wings, echoes of the past mixed with the tension of the present, a matter of improbable museums, Toby's and the one Grandfather never could or would create. Because while the old German pastor was quite proud of his work, his paintings were shut away in the third, never occupied, bedroom of the house, he said they were not good enough to be shown, to which Grandmother replied, You talk as if we country folk knew something about painting! And I recalled one morning under a fiery sky, after Grandfather had left for the church, she had taken the paintings out and exhibited them against the walls of the house and on our two longest tables, which we had to clear of clutter. We were in the middle of the 1980s or a little later, and Grandfather had kept the fifty-odd paintings he found acceptable. At about eight o'clock that morning, people Grandmother called My Guests began arriving, about twenty faces unfamiliar to me, including two blond-haired women who stood out, Nurses who've come from Namur to train the dispensary staff, Grandmother whispered, I thought they'd appreciate your grandfather's works. And I also invited a few growers, some of the ones your grandfather painted, it will be interesting to see their reaction, don't you think? . . . And all those people filed past the paintings. They weren't very talkative, those people who got to see the preview, they walked with their hands behind their backs, the nurses sent by the king of the Belgians nodded approvingly and chirped, Interesting, interesting, such flamboyant colours! They repeated this drivel over and over, and, at all of eight or nine years old, I understood that they knew nothing about painting, adorable boors with foreheads burned by the sun of our plateaus and, it could very well be that Bruegel the Elder was completely unknown to them and they were unable to make a connection between Grandfather's work and his. The peasants Grandmother had invited stood motionless in front of the oils, charcoals, and gouaches, expressionless, even in front of the series the artist had titled "Peasant Gazes," six portraits intended to reveal the happiness hidden behind the dull, reddened eyes of the coarse farm people. I recall that three tenant farmers, kind souls, had come to pose for Grandfather, and while he was painting they had kept twiddling their thumbs in boredom or resignation, so that in the end what was painted was less the happiness in the eyes of the country people than the resignation and stoicism of peasant misery posing for a mad painter. So the peasant visitors to the temporary museum had stood in front of those painted images of themselves gazing back at them—what a fabulous mirror is art!—and they seemed to be wondering, What is the difference between these persons confined in images and us? Who is free, them or us?

This whole charade lasted a good hour. Grandmother had prepared lemongrass tea and bean fritters, which were appreciated by the nurses and growers, who had built up an appetite from their art expedition. After nine o'clock, Grandfather walked up the little hill to the house with his cane, and he tensed when he saw the intruders. Annoyed, he asked, What are you doing? Grandmother gave him some tea, while the nurses came over timidly to congratulate him. It's just a hobby, Grandfather answered. As for the growers, they greeted the pastor and not the artist, frozen smiles on their faces.

24

THIS TIME TOBY TOOK A MACHETE out of his bottomless bag. He said it had belonged to his friend Sango. That during the night Sango had run amok and laid waste to his last cotton plants. At night, so as to hide his shame, to hide from the sun the piece of shit he had become, reduced to prowling around Old Bisko's seed mill, where a few women still came to grind the remnants of maize and millet they had miraculously discovered in the bottom of the granaries. At night, too, because Sango no longer believed in the light of a deceptive dawn. Because in the daytime the mocking yellow disc of the sun exposed his ill fortune. At night, to try to still exist through actions that the violence of the sun would not annihilate. At the end of the day Sango, armed with a trowel and a plastic bag, would go to the mill to recover from the dirt floor the flour dropped from the women's basins, and Old Bisko, looking at him with sad eyes, would sometimes give him a paltry cob to roast in his backyard. He told Bisko he wanted to go away, to cross the desert and then the Mediterranean and find a childhood friend in Spain. The latest news was that Sango had called Old Bisko from Libya and told him it was hell.

That was three months ago, said Toby, hanging the machete on the wall using a hole drilled in the wooden handle. He said that later he would recover other peasants' tools for his museum, and seeds too, from the rarest to those of cashew, kapok, kola, and eucalyptus plants, which were still part of the landscape of our plains, valleys, mountains, and towns. He should also, he thought, try to find out what had become of the only son of the former corporal Yambo, the bag maker, who was said to have gone to the big city, and try to learn the fate of the bags and the earth they contained. Because, as for the corporal himself, it was clear from the outset that he would one day pass away alone in the mire, dying like a miserable abandoned mutt. But Toby wondered what had happened to the bags of earth. He picked up his lighter again. —Sorry, Robinson, I have to do it for Yambo, I've got to burn you. —Think! I shouted. If I'm dead, you're dead too! —Aren't you listening, Toby? Ed cried. Don't touch your hostage! You'll only make your case worse! I'm telling you again that serious discussions have begun with The Firm. —There's nothing to discuss! said Toby. Transfer the money and we'll be quits! Well, almost. You care about your friend, don't you? . . . The overseer James Hoogan said to Winnie a few minutes before the execution, I see that you care about that dog, Samuel. It's only normal, bitches care about dogs. . . . But Hoogan had a brain the size of a testicle and he couldn't know that Winnie had long understood that a Samuel or Robert in chains sometimes had to die to establish the power and beauty of the great work and ensure that it endured forever.

23

I TOLD TOBY HE WAS NO ONE'S SPOKESPERSON, that he was alone, a Robin Hood of the savannahs self-appointed in the indifference of the time and of living creatures, I told him his little action had the sole aim of coming to the rescue of his Ruth of Savannah, who must be in a difficult situation. Admit that your grower friends didn't ask you to do any of this, Toby! Are you ashamed to admit that at the centre of all this there's nothing but your Ruth? That phantom you talk to in your delirium? Because you know you can't save the world from monsters like The Firm, you want to at least try to do something for your girlfriend from Georgia. Admit I'm right! —Are you playing mind reader now, Robinson? Don't stick your nose into this. Ruth didn't ask anyone for anything! —Is she cute? Brilliant? Stupid? —Shut up! You're getting on my nerves! I'll gag you and burn you if you're not careful with your adjectives when you talk about Ruth! She's anything but dumb. He sat down again against the wall and told me that two years ago, five months after he had started growing Bt cotton, he had received a letter from The Firm informing him that he had been selected to participate in an organized trip with a group of a dozen prominent growers. Did he want to be in on the adventure? Destination Georgia, in the American South that had made cotton a miracle, mountains of white gold in the fields around Savannah, Smithville, Albany, etc. The Firm was going to introduce them to a miracle, a miracle they too could create in their savannahs. Toby said he wasn't thrilled at first. What miracle was The Firm talking about, the one of Black slaves lined up all season long between rows of white fibre, the whip of an impatient overseer on their backs?

He said the Miracle was named Ruth. When he was a librarian, he had discovered the deep South in books, stories of pioneers, bloody battles and short-lived victories by the Indian chief Tomochichi, the Marquis de Lafayette, Confederate or Union soldiers, General Lee, and all the Savannah ghosts who had died of yellow fever. It was anything but a dream or a miracle, it was Margaret Mitchell's novel *Gone with the Wind* and the film, and another book and film too, *Midnight in the Garden of Good and Evil*, which he had gone to see in the movie theatre with a date one night, he said, And it was really great, Robinson, very good acting by Kevin Spacey in the role of the antique dealer Jim Williams. Once I got past my initial skepticism, I was quite curious to discover the South. I wanted to see the miracle in my own fields, and The Firm was taking care of the visa formalities and all that stuff. —So you had a nice trip to Georgia at the expense of the Monster? —Affirmative. I went to stretch my legs on the other side of the Atlantic. My first flight outside this continent, I must say. On the recommendation of the salesman for The Firm, that strange character Zak Bolton, I was one of some dozen growers in whom, I learned, they had supposedly identified what is known as leadership potential. In short, guys who, on their return from America, would help convince more peasants to get on board with Bt cotton, influencers, to use a trendy term.

And so there they were in Georgia on a pleasant August afternoon, lodged in a modest but chic hotel on River Street, one of those former cotton warehouses of the Savannah riverfront converted into new establishments for various purposes. Their guide, a pudgy guy with a full, completely white beard, as voluble as a sideshow barker, had teased them, Dear African growers, you're staying in an old cotton warehouse, it's a sign that you'll be the new factors, or brokers, and the bourgeoisie of cotton! I suggest that, after you've had a nap, you join me in the lobby of the hotel for a first tour on the ballast stones trodden long ago by the pioneers of cotton. . . . The next day, the group, accompanied by the brash guide and two other employees, went to The Firm's offices ten minutes from downtown Savannah, a building with a grey façade of rough cement, quite a gloomy place; however that wasn't the worst thing about it. A few minutes later, in an appallingly air-conditioned conference room, the Black growers were treated to a course on Bt cotton given by a fashion model in a clinging loud blue outfit. The model, whose body was as dry as a stalk maize at harvest time, rattled off her lesson on things transgenic in a voice like a train whistle, and they were given pens and big notebooks to take notes. Half the growers, who were no longer used to such an activity, had by mutual agreement begun to chew on the ends of the Montblanc pens, while the dried-up maize stalk went on to chapter two, on preparing the soil for seeding.

Toby went on, getting angry, They gave us their spiel on the revolution represented by Bollgard Bt cotton seed, the peasants it had saved in India, in China, and in wonderful America, where we now happened to be, the virtues of Roundup, the pesticide blessed by all the Greek and Roman gods of fertility, the need to follow the production process to the letter, from seeding, field maintenance, and spraying herbicides, to harvest. And the maize stalk, illuminated by the thousand fires of the agricultural revolution, had finished her spiel in French after a good hour, with the presentation of world statistics—Bullshit! said Toby—showing that the cotton harvest increased threefold while the effort required was reduced by ninety percent. One of the representatives of The Firm addressed them, concluding his speech with this sublime thought: Here in the South we have faced up to our history. Once, Black slaves were exploited in the cotton fields; today, you who come from the same continent are the princes of that same cotton. . . . Toby remembered that their guide, whose name was Tom, had chuckled softly from his seat in a corner of the room.

After this introduction, they were treated in the afternoon to a short visit to a farm where field trials had been carried out, a half hour during which Toby felt that the head scientist was being vague and that he twitched nervously at the slightest question from his guests from the savannahs of the dark continent. They had understood absolutely nothing about the process of hybridization of seeds, but had appreciated the green beauty of the cotton plants, which were handled with meticulous care. Toby was exhausted, all he wanted was to lean back, a beer in his hand, against the huge trunk of a century-old oak he had noticed when their chartered bus crossed Bull Street. The next day, they visited another farm, where perfectly straight rows of cotton plants stretched as far as the eye could see. For two long hours, the Georgia grower had showered Bollgard with praise.

As they were leaving the farm, they encountered Ruth and her group at the front gate. Ruth in the middle of some dozen rowdy protestors carrying placards that read: *The Firm is killing our planet! Bollgard is a monster! Stop the crime against nature!* Ruth with her energetic movements, which Toby had immediately noticed, like a tornado roiling the dull order and calm of things before his amazed eyes. Ruth, her red hair laced with a few strands of silver, her eyes green as a field in the sun, her mouth, the full lips spitting a stream of foul words in the faces of The Firm's representatives. The protesters were preventing the members of the delegation from getting to their bus, and the agents of The Firm in charge of the security of men and GMOs intervened to push them out of the way, Move! You're on private property! And when the frightened visitors had finally found an opening through which they could get out and the whole delegation was rushing to get on the bus, Toby had lingered for several long seconds in front of the scene of citizens up in arms against The Firm. He had been struck by those eyes green as a field, with their flashes of anger. They're lying! he understood the woman to be saying in her accent, the anger in her eyes turning her cheeks red. The bus was ready to leave. He was the last one left to board. But he had just realized that he had been waiting for those eyes his whole pathetic life, and dead Samuel Brown had never again seen the loving eyes of Winnie, to whom Pastor Bill had said, The ways of God are inscrutable. Samuel with cracks and craters in his back, Samuel with thousands of wounds, wells drilled, in which you could make out something like a liquid, water or oil or some other precious miracle.

22

3:36 PM. WE ONCE AGAIN HEARD the distant hum of the air conditioning. I crossed my fingers. Toby looked me in the eye and said dreamily,
We're not alone, Robinson. Elsewhere in the world, far and near, there
are millions of people who support our cause. —You mean you're not
alone because there are a lot of you? You're wrong. —Always so negative.
You'll die alone and forgotten by everyone in whatever rotten corner
of France, Switzerland, or Belgium you lay your head. —Germany,
Toby. —What's the difference? It's all the same capitalist hell. —As you
wish, but I won't die alone. We're going to croak together today. He went
to glance out the window. I noted that he never spent more than two
or three seconds there, to the right or left of the window frame, with
his head lowered, as if he was trying to avoid the whistling bullet of an
unseen sniper positioned high in the surrounding area. When he came
back, he was anxious. He said, I saw him, Robinson. The angel—or the
devil, if you wish. Zak Bolton, the ambassador of The Firm. You know,
the guy who sold me on Bt cotton. He's here, standing a bit back from
the group in front of the entrance. —Are you sure? He returned to the
window again, and then came back. He's not there anymore, he said, but
I swear on the graves of my old parents, I saw him!

I focused my attention on the sounds of the people outside, which
we could hear in the distance even though the street of the museum
must have been closed off, we could hear them from our lair. A group
of people, the crowd in a market or in a public place has an energy,
Grandfather used to say, After all, what are Bruegel's paintings of

peasant dances and weddings about if not the beauty of energy, movement, and colour? . . . It was near the end of the 1980s, Grandfather was still filling the house with paintings under Grandmother's puzzled gaze. Energy, my lad, nothing but that, Grandfather repeated. The fire in their movements, you see, that's what I've tried to represent on this canvas. . . . He had painted a scene of a weighing in the yard of the former Colonial Cotton Company, renamed the Gulf Cotton Company eight years after independence was won by thugs, including a sergeant from the colonial army, who had seized power in a bloodbath. The scene of the weighing, the newly picked cotton packed in the burlap we call cotokou, a bale a metre and a half in diameter tied by two pairs of strong hands, which were shown in one of the paintings of the series. Grandfather asked, Do you feel the energy in those fingers that have to pull the edges of the burlap hard in order to be able to tie them together? Do you feel that combination of dexterity and energy? Yes, Grandfather, I answered. He looked deep into my eyes, both happy and fearful, to see to what extent I shared his madness, how much I believed in his work. He followed my gaze, which had shifted to another canvas of the series on energy, the workers, muscular arms bare and glistening with sweat now lifting the bale as if to offer it to the gods of the harvest, the energy, the four pairs of outstretched arms straining under the load as round as the Earth, and Grandfather had commented, That's how those peasants carry our world with the strength of their arms. But it was just a big bale bursting with that white fibre given by Providence or by a strange demon who amused himself sometimes by being generous, the bale lifted and hung on an antique scale with an old copper disc, a valuable dynamometer attached to the middle of a heavy rafter whose ends rested on crumbling cement beams in the yard of the Cotton Company. The next painting showed the bale hanging from the rusted hook of the scale, with hands laid on the belly of the huge sack to stabilize it so as to get the exact weight. It seemed to me now that I'd seen those scenes and those people in real life more than in the drawings and oils by Grandfather, who now, in the late 1980s, was quite happy with his series on peasant energy, although he said, It seems that all that magnificent energy will little by little be swallowed by machines, metal in place of hearts and hands. But don't they say you can't stop progress? But what progress is there if the heart is no longer in it, if the growers, overcome by crickets, sparse rain, and debt, are no longer anything but worn-out shadows moving wearily, lost in burned furrows? . . . And as an adolescent full of doubts, I wondered, will we now see the festive energy of sowing and harvesting only in painters' canvases?

I was to ask myself that question again many years later, in Jinshan, on the outskirts of Shanghai, where I discovered a peasant painting in bright colours depicting ripe fields, village or market squares, orange dragons, and yellow birds flying above the heads of people sitting at tables. I spent a week in Jinshan trying to identify what led the artists of that region, too, to paint simplicity, laughter, and celebration, with figures blowing with all their might into some kind of horns, raising outstretched arms victoriously to a sky filled with fireworks. I was disoriented, lost, because the journalist that I am was running after peasant distress and desperation, which to my regret had become my stock-in-trade. I had to seek what was ugly, painful, cruel. As I travelled farther from Jinshan into the countryside, I met growers who, despite the fact that they were harvesting almost nothing, continued to smile under the blue sky. And I couldn't say that the heavens were laughing at their apparent innocence.

I SAW HIM! REPEATED TOBY. Zak Bolton, the imp in the skin of an angel selling cotton seed! It was him, no doubt about it! The angel or the devil in a suit and a felt hat is an American merchant of dreams. Toby sat down again against the wall and began describing the man to me, The day that guy appeared in front of me, I didn't hear him coming, although I was sitting on the patio of our house at the edge of the fields. I looked up from my account book with its negative numbers and I saw him, I didn't hear his footsteps on the gravel path leading to the patio. As I told you, the dandy wore an impeccably pressed suit that captured all the light of the morning sky, a green necktie, a gray felt hat pulled down over his eyebrows, his lean, fine-featured face extended by a perfect white goatee I couldn't help admiring. After introducing himself, he said, Not very good, those numbers, are they, Toby? But if you want, we can fix that. . . . And in five short minutes, leaning on one of the pillars of the patio, he served up his sermon on Bt cotton to a suspicious Toby.

Toby drank from his gourd and held it out to me, saying, I've only tied your wrists, you can still grab it in your hands, can't you? I reluctantly swallowed a mouthful of water while Toby continued his story, That guy Zak Bolton was like a magician. When we met again a few days later, he sat down across from me on the patio and, in the calm, soft voice of a messenger from the beyond, with his long fingers outlining the miracle of the world of the future where I would only have to snap my fingers to harvest the cotton, he managed to take me in. I was watching a magic trick, the persuasive words he pulled out of his sleeve, a series of adjectives—fabulous, extraordinary, shining, sublime, etc—floated briefly in the warm air before permanently taking root in me, cancelling all my attempts to counter them. And after the words, the magician angel pulled from his other sleeve the incredible numbers and statistics I told you about, Robinson. That's what it was, a magic trick, so I later wondered if I had actually chosen to go into Bt cotton. That's what my grower friends also say, we can't say we chose, it just happened. . . . At the end of the meeting, Toby had shaken the hand of the devil with the manner of an angel, who had looked into his eyes, their hands still locked together. —Robinson, it was as if we were signing a pact. I thought I saw something like a flash of warning in that weird fellow's eyes. When he finally let go of my hand, I felt troubled and I went right back into the house to protect myself from lightning or an evil spell.

His hands trembled, he hugged himself and said, Yes, I signed a pact with Lucifer. And all sorts of misfortunes befell me because I didn't respect the terms of that agreement. —What do you mean? —I got Zak Bolton's damn seed. I had to give him something in exchange. —Oh, yeah? You paid for your seed. —It's not a question of money. I was punished for my lack of faith, I never really believed in their miracle cotton. —They couldn't force you to believe in it. —I know, but there was our pact. Do you know the story of the movie *Crossroads*, Walter Hill, 1986? —So that's it, Toby. You've watched too many movies. Is it an American story? —Yes. I told you, the angel or the devil is American. —You're raving, Toby. Is it fatigue? —No. In *Crossroads*, an old harmonica player promises a young guitar player who loves the blues that he'll give him the lost thirtieth song by bluesman Robert Johnson if he'll drive him to Mississippi; he confesses that at a young age he signed a pact with the Devil. And he ended up miserable. Like me. The Devil had the same face as our Zak Bolton. If you want to do business with him, you have to believe and obey. From the start, I didn't take that guy and his cronies from The Firm seriously.

I only went along with their deal out of frustration. And our trip to Georgia, land of the princes of cotton, I also took that lightly. As a result, I was punished. —You're exhausted, Toby. —Maybe. That must be it. But there's something that doesn't add up. That ghost Zak Bolton.

And he told me that during the disaster the growers had prayed, the flock had made a desperate appeal to Allah the Merciful and his Prophet. They added hymns and the gospel story that's been read and discussed a thousand times, the story in which Christ multiplied the loaves and fed thousands of empty bellies. There were also some who turned to other divinities that were invisible or had bodies of clay, over which they poured offerings of palm oil and libations of fresh blood in which the cotton boll had been dipped to rid it of the evil eye. Toby continued, Only Wali, my hanged friend, didn't go into churches, temples, or mosques, he didn't believe in those things of faith. . . . Like Toby himself, who in these times of piety had taken refuge in the dives and clandestine saloons of the capital to raise his glass to the health of that god who didn't exist for him. Who didn't exist, because he, Toby, was not humble or crazy enough to create him through the endless repetition of kowtows, hymns, psalms, and genuflections. And because Wali didn't believe in any of that either, he had chosen to depart at the end of his rope one bright morning, he had left the scene of dead cotton before a wily, treacherous god could come and keep him alive in his fields any longer and continue to make a fool of him.

Those unhappy children of cotton, said Toby, came back exhilarated from the prayer sessions because rooted in them they had a profound conviction that America, its gods, and its corporations could not be malicious. Hadn't America been good and generous with the Blacks, sending them its Peace Corps volunteers to calm their passion for war in Biafra or Katanga, America the champion of humanitarianism, distributing food in our miserable shantytowns, vegetable oil, biscuits, canned goods, bars of soap, bags of short-grain rice shipped by boat to the ports of the continent, medical supplies, immaculate bandages and compresses generously provided to our phantom hospitals?

Sorry, Robinson, to get the Americans of The Firm to budge, I have to be mean. . . . Toby holding the lighter with the little flame in his fist, I frozen in my corner waiting for the torture, and an uncaring crowd of people in the photographs. —Don't be stupid, Toby, I finally said, my temples throbbing. And Ed yelled, No, Toby! Don't start again, Toby! Someone from The Firm should call you soon, meanwhile keep away from your hostage. —Someone? But I didn't ask to speak to anyone. I want our bank transfer, that's all! Obviously, you're not taking me seriously, and that's too bad. The next moan you hear will be that of a dying man! —Toby, if you'd been able for an instant to get into your head Winnie's thoughts, you'd have understood that the agonies, the Achilles tendons cut or the nails driven into the skull, were nothing compared to the beauty of the great work. On the contrary, the torture was to ensure its impact, and Winnie was still unhappy with the fact that the great work was not only beautiful, it was undeniably useful too, because it ensured the privileges and the glory of empires, kingdoms, and countries like that of the overseer James Hoogan.

3:59 PM. TOBY STOPPED IN FRONT of a few photos and spent a good minute in front of the rope of Wali, the man who had hanged himself. He picked up the bottle of dirty water, and put it back on the display stand after studying it with clinical attention as if he had just discovered it. In Georgia, too, he said, they wreaked havoc. . . . Two days after the episode at the farm on the outskirts of Savannah, he had again seen the woman with red hair and eyes like a field in spring. He was walking in the old town of Savannah, around various squares, enjoying the vegetation that reminded him of home, dwarf palms and palmyra palms in the sun, the houses from another time, Victorian mansions, their porticos with Doric columns, their wrought-iron balconies, fences, and gates. He was about to sit down on one of the wooden benches in Monterey Square when she approached, striding confidently toward him, and said right off, You looked out of sorts during your visit to the farm the other day. Don't tell me The Firm forced you to make this journey to our Old South? Would you like to have coffee with me? I have things to tell you.

And Toby had gone with his hostess, who led the way with assurance through the crowd of tourists and retired people ambling along with their hands behind their backs or leaning against the powerful trunks of the oak trees, fingering the Spanish moss hanging from the branches. They walked through Wright Square, where Toby was only able to catch a glimpse of the marble flagstones placed in memory of the illustrious founders of the city. Ruth, beside whom he was walking now in silence, said, If they had to provide stones and statues for all those who have made this city, we wouldn't know where to put our feet anymore. . . . They ended up in a tiny bistro in an alley whose name Toby didn't remember. After they had ordered, she had looked into his eyes and said, You come from far away, don't you? Africa? But you're not going to let yourself be taken in by the sorcerer's apprentices from The Firm? You know, the little farm they showed you has nothing to do with reality. Those fields you saw, well, they had to be weeded by hand! I suppose they didn't tell you it's hell for them now with our beautiful amaranth? —Amaranth? —Amaranth, she said, blowing on her coffee. Let's just say that, for our part, we're quite pleased. They didn't manage to get rid of the amaranth with their damn pesticide, Roundup. That nasty plant just keeps spreading, it's a real nightmare for the cotton growers. And they all curse it, our superweed that's capable of taking root deep in the ground, making any attempt to pull it out an ordeal. There was a transfer of genes between the amaranth and the modified seeds that made it resistant to spraying with pesticides. It has really slowed down The Firm's plans these last few months. But for how long, you might ask. You'll excuse me for approaching you like this, but you could have refused to plant their Roundup Ready in the fields where you come from. You would have saved yourselves a lot of problems. But tell me a little about yourself. Toby didn't say a word, preferring to keep listening to her rant against The Firm, watching her lips moving nervously, her cheekbones golden with the fire of her red mane, her nostrils flaring with each sally against The Firm, the green of her eyes that seemed to preserve the innocence and carefree quality of a time long past. He simply smiled. She pursed her lips and asked, You think it's funny? —No, he said, I find you fascinating with your boldness and your ardour. Could it be that you were born on the day of a tornado in this fabled South? She smiled and looked away, and Toby was afraid of losing the green field, the ultimate land of innocence he had glimpsed. She confronted him again, You aren't taking me seriously. —I didn't say that. —Believe me, The Firm is not sowing the seeds of happiness all over the place. —Why do you want to warn me? —Our paths have crossed, I'd never have forgiven myself if I hadn't warned you. —You're very kind. —It's not kindness. I'm just trying as best I can to throw a bit of sand into The Firm's works. And if I can, to convince you to give up their Bt cotton, you or someone else. She looked away again. Toby had scored his first point, and he smiled and said, And you hoped to convince me in the time it took to have a coffee? You're very sure of yourself. —We're trying to act as quickly as possible, I and the friends you saw two days ago at that farm. —What are you doing tomorrow? —Why? —I told you, you can't expect to convince me with just one coffee.

She didn't answer, she went back to the amaranth, ranting, To deal with our resistant plant, The Firm encouraged the growers to increase the applications of Roundup. Roundup contains glyphosate, a nasty carcinogen. Around Charleston and Albany, in the communities that live near the fields of GMO crops, substantial increases in the numbers of people with lymphoma, leukemia, and prostate cancer have been observed. And as if that weren't enough, because Roundup turned out to be powerless against amaranth, the sorcerers from The Firm encouraged the farmers to use another pesticide, awful stuff, 2,4-D. Do you see what's going on? —No. But call me Toby, he said. He couldn't take his eyes off her mobile, hungry lips. —Ruth Jefferson. —So what is 2,4-D? —Well, it's an ingredient in Agent Orange, the diabolical herbicide the American army sprayed on the fields and forests of Vietnam for some ten years, between 1961 and 1971. The purpose? To starve the poor Vietnamese combatants. But it was mainly villages, communities, an entire people we screwed. That bloody defoliant, Agent Orange, which contains dioxins that persist in the environment for a long time, I mean years. —You know quite a bit about it, Ruth. —It's nasty shit. Right now as we speak, there are children being born in those parts of Asia we sprayed with our orange monster who have multiple birth defects, kids with deformed bodies, without arms, blind. With 2,4-D, The Firm is doing it again, creating a hell in the heart of our green fields. . . . The green fields were her eyes, that's what I said to her, Robinson. —So? —So, what? —How did she take it? —She laughed for an instant and, squeezing my forearm, told me to get rid of all the seeds The Firm had peddled to me. —Too late, I replied. —In that case, destroy everything as soon as you get home! —I have debts, Ruth. I'll have to see later. —You won't come out any better with their Bt cotton!

She told him she was from Anniston, Alabama. Her eyes glazed over. My family left Anniston back in the 1970s when The Firm dumped PCBs in the rivers. My mother didn't want me to be born in an area befouled with those toxic chlorine derivatives. And she ended up here. —It seems The Firm is following you. . . . She said that with amaranth the gods of the Native American peoples were taking revenge on The Firm. The Firm's pesticides couldn't destroy amaranth because it was the plant of the Inca, Aztec, and Maya gods. But we know that when the gods took revenge, they weren't always very selective, which is why innocent children would be born with horrible tails in the middle of their foreheads. Which is why we're all going to raise our glasses in a toast, Toby! We massacred the Native Americans and took over their lands. Today we've set in motion the process of destroying those same lands, until all that's left, stuck under the fingernails that extend from our skeletons, is traces of moon dust. Night is falling. Do you want to visit the real Savannah?

TOBY STUDIED THE IMAGE HE HAD TAKEN down from the wall, looking at it wryly. It was an old charcoal drawing, not a photograph. He laughed. Here's something you'll really enjoy. He took apart the frame protecting the drawing and came back over to me with the fragile piece of paper, which was about seventy by fifty centimetres in size. The label he had removed from the frame read "Cotton gin, Charleston, South Carolina, 1797, artist unknown, work on loan from The Foundation." The cotton gin, which had a drum with teeth between two strong boards set vertically, was being worked by a group of slaves, one turning the crank of the machine while another fed the white fibre into it between the drum and some small hooked cylinders. A woman was walking toward them carrying a basket of cotton on her head. Toby fumed, Are they trying to tell us that this machine was of some use to the slaves? —This is a museum, Toby. I can understand that they wanted to show everything related to cotton. —You don't get it, Robinson. I don't think those men and women you see around this lovely invention have any desire to celebrate. Do you really believe the cotton gin made the work of the slaves easier? Well, it didn't! The slave trade, which had been petering out, picked up again strongly in the American South, because more slaves were needed to satisfy the ghoulish appetite of the gin! So you'll understand why I'm so eager to get rid of this thing, which is horribly offensive to me!

He returned to the window. A few seconds later, the paper was on fire in the harsh air of the afternoon and the turacos were flying frightened, astray in the sky of the city, and Samuel Brown in the pillory hadn't seen any birds in the Alabama sky while the overseer's dogs were growling around his dangling legs, perhaps he thought his skin, like the land, could regenerate in the course of the seasons, fresh weeds growing from his pores, and Toby dropped to the floor against the wall beside the shutters, through which came the outraged voice of Ed Kaba, telling him again that he was making things worse for himself, that the exhibition could still be saved, that he would like to send water and fruit to me. —Bullshit! cried Toby, we have everything we need, we're sharing the same gourd of fresh water. —But he must be hungry! —I don't think so. He agrees with me that the situation is too serious for him to be wasting time stuffing his face! Don't wait too long before you remedy my grievance and you may be able to see him alive again. —You've already done enough damage, Toby!

Ed was silent and, for the first time since I was taken hostage, I thought about my body. I had never been able to eat much in the morning, and I should mention that at one point while I was walking through the exhibition hall I had gone to relieve my bladder. Which is why my body had not yet called on me to eliminate the waste products of what I had consumed. But if I kept on drinking from Toby's gourd, I would soon suffer biological consequences that would be regrettable for my honour. I asked, Who told you I wasn't hungry, Toby? —Let's say I assumed it, Robinson. You know this isn't a dinner date. In our position, we should be satisfied with a few swallows of water from time to time. But if you want to be served a meal, I can poke around in my bag. —I'm very demanding in terms of gastronomy. —You don't know what I have in my bag. —I know all too well! Let me go, Toby! I'm sore all over and I'm mad as hell at you! You can see your plan isn't working! They're not going to pay!

Toby didn't reply. He took some more things out of his bag and came back and sat down cross-legged facing me. He put a pile of documents in the hollow of his legs, cleared his throat, and said in a serious, professorial tone, What would a museum be without important original texts and documents, Robinson? So here they are. This first paper is one of the promotional texts The Firm distributed touting its Bt cotton. You may admire that overly green field and those suspiciously large cotton bolls. And what do we read here? "With Bt cotton, no more worries, no more debts, no more hours of hard labour in the fields." This envelope contains another document, it's the letter our group of growers sent to The Firm when the dream turned into a nightmare, expressing our disappointment and anger and denouncing the horrible lies we were victims of. The letter had been returned to them with no explanation. —It's a postal mystery, Robinson, a letter returned for no reason. The diligent representatives of The Firm hadn't even bothered to read it. We didn't open it, but here's the copy we made. Let's continue. Here are three blank pages I'm going to exhibit. They represent the answers we never received from The Firm or from our wonderful authorities. They also represent the silence the growers have been reduced to. . . . I congratulated Toby for his appropriately even-handed approach. He roared, Are you going to take me seriously? —Let's say I'm trying to lighten the mood. —Spare me your comments. All I ask is that you listen to me. Here are three of the growers' account books. Their numbers were down to rock bottom. And I also have some harassing letters from our creditors. Will you help me label all this stuff before I put it up on the display stands? —No. —Why not?

He said he was feeling inspired to describe the new items, I'm on fire, Robinson! I've been visited by the gods. Don't you feel their protective spirit all around us? —The gods have abandoned you, Toby. —I have nothing to say to that. So, for The Firm's promotional rag, I'll write "One of the fraudulent brochures The Firm produced for the growers." For the letter, it will be "The growers' letter that was returned to them with no explanation," and we'll add "Sheer contempt." For the blank sheets, it will be "The blank pages of powerlessness and silence. By Toby Kunta." —You're not very modest, Friday. —Don't call me that! I'm not the native in a goddamn novel! —Well, The Firm treats you like a worthless native. He said the blank sheets were his idea, and he was entitled to put his name on them. Or else people wouldn't understand. —Hats off to the artist! —For the account books, let's just put "The accounts of defeat and ruin." And at the end I write, "Hell was the harassing letters from creditors." —Nice work, Toby! —Are you laughing at me again? Enough joking around, it's obvious that if I want to get my two hundred million, I have to go through with this. For sure it's going to hurt, Robinson. . . . The lighter reappeared in his hands. I cried, Don't be stupid! And Ed shouted, Toby, calm down, they should be making you a proposal shortly. And let me repeat that this exhibition is important, for the peasants, for the country, for The Firm and its partners who support our agriculture. —What a load of crap! There won't be any exhibition! In conclusion, Mr Director, the odds that your friend will return home tonight are becoming very slim, almost zero!

I REMEMBERED THE TIME I returned home with some lines from a very fine poem by Senghor in which, at the end, he evokes his ancestors:

> *They call us the men of cotton of coffee of oil*
> *They call us the men of death.*
> *We are the men of dance, whose feet*
> *regain strength by pounding the hard ground.*

I read the poem to my grandparents, trying to memorize parts of it, and Grandfather left the bench facing the mountains where the three of us were sitting and went to his room to get a book, a beautiful antique volume with a yellowed cover. He opened it to page 36 in the section on the painters of the Flemish Renaissance, and there, between a portrait of a weaver by Maarten van Heemskerck and the hell painted by Hieronymus Bosch, was Bruegel's *Peasant Dance*. Passing his trembling hand again and again over the reproduction of the painting, Grandfather said, Like Bruegel, your Senegalese poet understood what we are, what we are beyond our destiny as people of the land, what we are beyond the harvests, the wine consumed or the palm oil produced. What, years later, the things exhibited in the Museum of Rural Life in Castellbisbal, in Catalan country, would tell me. What an ancient fireplace, cast iron cauldrons, winnowing baskets, an oil press, and an old metal brazier that warmed the modest peasant dwellings would tell me. The story of labour and of little joys told by the red earth of Castellbisbal, which was the same as that of the plateaus where I grew up. I went there from Lleida one cool morning in June, on the road that also led to Martorell, I drove fast, impatient because pieces of the puzzle that were to help me understand were waiting for me there.

HIS EYES FIXED ON A DISTANT SCENE beyond the walls of the exhibition hall and the things in it, Toby told me of his nocturnal tour of
Savannah with Ruth, the activist with the fiery mane. At around seven
in the evening, she had taken him to see her friend Ola Wiwa, the cook
at a modest restaurant in a brick building on River Street. Ola was waiting for them outside, in front of the business, leaning against a lamp-
post, smoking a cigarette. Ruth made the introductions. Ola blew smoke
towards a shooting star and said, I'm still jet-lagged, Princess Ruth. I got
back from Onitsha two days ago. Shall we go inside? My break is over.
Would you like to taste my yam and mutton stew? I can't say my customers detest it. You'll tell me what you think of it, Toby, you'll confirm,
or not, whether I make it as well as they do back there in your savannahs. . . . Ruth cleared her throat and interjected, But you won't forget
the main reason I brought him here to you, right? —No way, Princess!
I'll finish my shift in two hours and we'll go initiate our guest. Toby
raised an eyebrow. Ruth laughed, You're not afraid, I hope? —No, said
Toby. But I take a pass when it comes to initiations. My last one goes
back to my circumcision. She blushed and went ahead of them into an
inner room painted completely black. She whispered to Toby, The darkness reassures the good spirits of this city that come here.

All the tables in the restaurant were taken, except the one Ruth had
reserved. The mutton stew lived up to the promises. While Ruth was
asking him a thousand questions about life in his country on the savannahs, Toby couldn't take his eyes off her mouth as her eager lips received

the food. She squeezed his hand and asked him if he had thought about it. —About what, Ruth? —About the Bt cotton. Are you going to pull out? —I think I'll try one or two more seasons, until I've made enough to pay off my debts. —You're very stubborn. Ola also thinks it's a mistake. —My back is to the wall, Ruth. —Come on, there may be surprises in store for you. —What kind of surprises? You amaze me. I thought you only believed in action? —You just die if you don't have a little faith. And sometimes, you meet someone. . . . They couldn't take their eyes off each other. Ola came and asked, What else would you like, my friends? Eat well, the night is long. Especially tonight.

Afterwards they got into Ola's rickety Ford, and after speeding through the sleepy streets for a quarter of an hour they arrived at an old bungalow south of the city. Sitting on the front steps with another person was a matronly woman who looked like an ogress and whose hair in the darkness appeared to be grey. They didn't greet each other; Ruth had whispered to Toby that these people were concentrating in preparation for entering another world. They didn't linger in the living room, but went down to a basement with walls painted white. The matronly woman sat down in an armchair at the far end of the room, a chair that appeared to be immaculately white despite the dim light in the place. In the right-hand corner behind her stood a wooden object about one metre sixty high, with a carved knob. Toby said he understood it to be Ola's bocio, or guardian, the spirit protector of the place. The priestess took various objects from a canvas bag she was holding at arm's length, including a little gourd filled with white powder, a statuette with a misshapen head, and a vial whose contents were a red that was almost brown. The man with her sat down on the old wood floor beside the white throne. After taking their shoes off and placing them along the wall behind them, Ola, Toby, and Ruth sat down facing the two. The priestess chanted some incomprehensible incantations, opened a bottle of water and added a little of it to the powder in the gourd, and poured the white liquid on the square of linoleum covering the floor in front of her, her lips moving again in esoteric chanting.

Then she spoke more clearly, calling on the spirits of the ancestors and thanking them with a gesture. She poured the contents of the vial on the head of the statuette. A smell of blood, which revolted Toby. Ruth maintained an impressive calm, absorbed in the ritual. The priestess said, This city belongs to ghosts. But there are some ghosts, those of slaves, that have been forgotten. In this cellar, I want to awaken them and invite them to join with the living, with the people of today, most of whom have forgotten those who built this country. I invoke them and I sense them already in our breathing. . . . While the priestess was speaking, her assistant struck a metal gong hanging from his hand with a piece of wood. The woman took a notebook from her bag and, with her eyes closed and her head nodding, began to draw on the pages. She emerged from her trance five minutes later, tore out the pages, and, smiling now, handed them to Ola, saying, Here are their faces, go and draw them on the walls and on anything you can in Savannah, beside the statues of our white gentlemen, slave owners, generals, heroes, and prophets. May all of Georgia and its cops who shoot Black people like they're rabbits remember that our Old South was also born of the blood spilled by those slaves in the fields.

Ten minutes later they were back out on the street. They said goodbye to the priestess and her acolyte, and as they got into the Ford, Toby ranted, Leave them in peace, those poor dead slaves! Ola drove towards downtown Savannah. They made stops of about ten minutes each at Reynold, Wright, Lafayette, Monterrey, Madison, Johnson, and finally, Chippewa Square. In each square, Ruth would hold a flashlight while Ola, armed with cans of spray paint, drew the faces of the slaves transmitted through the priestess on the trunks of the century-old oaks. Because Ola's thing was the trees, which he said were inhabited by spirits. Ten minutes to do each of the portraits of the anonymous dark-skinned men and women whose necks had borne the heavy yoke of captivity, Ola working with quick, precise movements while Ruth glanced around in case a police car poked its colourful nose in. Ola and Ruth, in the middle of the hot night of the South, worked on their spirit trees, art that would the next day be erased by agents of the city. Toby watched, sitting on the black stone edge of a fountain that sparkled with a thousand liquid lights, and Ruth took a photo of each one before they got back in the Ford. And Toby remembered, each of their transformed trees carried a name and a year: Thomas, 1734; Mary, 1699; Bob, 1745; Oscar, 1731; Louisa, 1697; John-Tiwa, 1765; Alice-Demilade, 1692; Rose-Chima, 1756; Enoch, 1759—the names and faces on the sheets of paper given to them by the priestess. Three times a year, at different hours so as not to fall into the traps laid by the police, Ola and Ruth carried out this action in the twenty-one squares of Savannah, and in the morning passersby and visitors could appreciate the tree-spirits, the tree-slaves, as they stood beside the copper plaques or statues honouring the combatants and mythic heroes of the slave-owning South. Toby had been puzzled by Ola and Ruth's devotion to this nocturnal action. He wondered what good they did, those dead faces on the immobile indifference of the trees.

Back in the Ford, Ruth took Toby's hand and squeezed it hard. She confided, For Ola, this ritual, this moment, is like a return to the land of his ancestors. Toby wanted to answer, Ola's ancestors forgot him a long time ago, and any return is a farce because you never return to the same place, and if Ola sometimes goes back to Onistha, it may just be to try to find his old loves.

A RETURN, JUNE 1990. At the insistence of his wife, Grandfather had decided to return to his birthplace. Grandmother had pestered him, What's the point of that German passport I got after my marriage if I can't go and see up close the place where you were born? . . . It was true that through my pastor forebear and my father I too was German, but in 1990, when I was twelve years old, you couldn't say I was in any great hurry to know the country of my ancestors, which was a distant world with vague outlines for me. However, one day in June 1990, I landed on the banks of the Weser with my grandparents—who had invested a good part of their savings in the trip—for what would be a one-month stay. We had lodgings in a hotel in the old city of Bremen; it was one of the tiny half-timbered dwellings in the area called Schnoor. Grandmother and I roamed around the city all day long, while Grandfather meditated in St Peter's Cathedral. On the second day, Grandfather, feeling a bit mischievous, played a trick on me. Not far from the market square there was a character dressed as a peasant woman with a drab dress and an off-white headdress. Pushing me towards her, Grandfather said, Go say hello to Gesche Gottfried, the poisoner! And instead of walking towards the public entertainer, who was offering cool—poisoned?—water from a pitcher, I ran away, giving Grandfather a good laugh. I remember that he had regained a kind of lightheartedness that contrasted with the serious air he always displayed on our plateaus. Our reactions, our curiosity as tourists newly arrived from the south must have been amusing to him. Standing with his hands behind his back, he let us go ahead to old buildings like the Brasilhaus, which had attracted our attention, or the Schifferhaus—the Shipper's House according to the brochure Grandmother took with her everywhere—which I ran to, wondering where were the ship and its captain, who I imagined with a pipe in his mouth. Or to the alleys, which were dark and so narrow that Grandmother and I could barely walk side by side without feeling we were melting into the grey stone of the dwellings.

That was how we spent most of our time in Bremen. In the second week we took the train to Tarmstedt, where Grandfather had spent his childhood on the family farm. He had one sister, who had died at the age of thirteen, when he was nearly ten. Grandfather managed to identify his parents' graves in a little village cemetery. He searched in vain for that of his sister in that realm of repose, where the oldest section merged with a field of barley reigned over by quiet blue birds. Grandfather remained motionless for several long minutes, his gaze fixed on the ripe golden barley. Grandmother shed a tear; did she understand then that it was not landscapes and scenes like those of Bruegel that he had been trying to paint, but rather the lost colours of his childhood? Yes, Grandmother was crying for those lost things we tried in vain to find in the pages of books, musical compositions, or paintings by Old Masters, struggling desperately against forgetting.

15

I RECALLED A PLEASANT AFTERNOON when Grandmother came to pick me up after school. We were walking hand in hand, they were taking Samuel Brown's hands out of the pillory, his dead body full of holes, a dry well, an exhausted mine, they were taking down that body they wouldn't hang again, unlike the body of Christ hanging in a corner of a chapel or on the pediment of a church, when the voice of Commissioner Shango rang out from the megaphone like the sound of a rusty machine, Toby, there's someone who wants to talk to you. —Sharing confidences isn't my thing, Commissioner. —I'm afraid you don't have a choice, Toby. Your cellphone will ring in two minutes. And you have to take that call, or else you alone will be responsible for what comes next. You care about the honour of your name, don't you? If you don't care that much about your skin, it seems to me your honour matters to you, at least a little. —I won't talk on the phone, Shango! —What if you did answer, Toby? I whispered. —You think I should, Robinson? —What are you risking? You never know. It's about to ring.

The cellphone rang. Toby froze. The device went silent, then rang again a minute later. Toby gave in with a sigh, Hello, yes? . . . As far as I'm concerned, things couldn't be better. I don't know who you are. I'd be surprised if we've met. What are you saying? Itiba? Itiba? That doesn't mean anything to me. You say Bijou is her whore name? It's possible I've crossed paths with a Bijou, yes. However, prostitutes aren't my thing. You're talking nonsense! Photos? What photos? Impossible. This is a crude setup! It can't be me! An hour to do what? If that's it, you can go ahead right away. Go on, show them to whoever you want, publish your photos! I'm not going to be taken in by an amateur like you! What a lousy parrot you make, my friend! Ciao. He hung up and remained lost in thought, his hand still clutching the device.

It looks like they have you by the balls, Friday! I said. —Don't call me Friday! —So what's happening? —Nothing, Robinson, absolutely nothing. I'm going back to work. I have to turn up the pressure a bit. —Out with it, Toby. I can tell you're getting really annoyed. —No big deal, Robinson. No big deal. —Tell me. Toby remained silent. —So? —If you insist! I know who Bijou is. But I'd bet my right arm she wasn't a whore. —How can you be so sure? —You can sense these things, Robinson. In the manner, the behaviour, the movements. She was really pretty, but very awkward. Which didn't displease me. —I see. You had a little fun with the girl one night. —We saw each other at least two evenings, Robinson. —So it was serious? —No. It was Ruth's fault. —Explain. —You have a talent for interrogation. Well, six months after I got back from Georgia, Ruth told me during one of our phone conversations that she didn't believe in long-distance relationships. She wanted us to stop calling each other. —So there was a relationship with Ruth. —I'm not a monk, Robinson! I really fell for her, my redhead from Savannah. So when she said she no longer wanted to—for a whole week, she didn't answer my calls or emails. Silence, Robinson, a horrible torture. One Saturday night, I went to Le Port, to the Makina Loka. You can imagine what followed. I was on my fifth Scotch when she sat down at my table. —Bijou? —Yes, all dolled up, full of the energy and sparkle of youth. I figured she was about twenty-three years old. And that was the first question that came to me through the haze of alcohol. I murmured, Let me guess your age, miss. If I hit it on the nose, you'll pay for my sixth Scotch. She agreed. I wasn't far off. Twenty-four, that's how old she said she was. After that I bought her a drink. She was hungry, so we went for a bite at Le Golfe. You know where that is, Robinson? —No. —It was a nice spread. The girl was really hungry. At one point during the meal, she looked into my eyes and said, I'm not a whore, Toby. The truth is that I'm in the red, in a bad spot, right at the beginning of the new university year. Can you help me out? I have to finish my master's in economics. I answered, And after that you'll come and save my finances as a cotton grower. Because, Bijou, things are looking bad for me financially. She pleaded, But can't you advance me something? —I could if I bled myself dry. You're a nice girl. —To thank you, I'd give you an unforgettable night. —You're not a prostitute, Bijou? —No. Let's say I'd like to comfort you. You look awfully sad and alone. Have you just been dumped? —Yes. But . . . —Hush! What would please you? —I don't know. —You have a day to think about it. Should I drop you at home? You're pretty wasted. —Tomorrow I'll give you the money. And yes, take me back to my hotel. And you're forbidden to come upstairs with me. I'm a gentleman. I don't take advantage of the first strange woman who sits down at my table. But if you have a car, couldn't you pay for your economics course? —A friend loaned it to me. —Well, well. That's what friends are for, huh?

The next night at seven, Bijou went to see Toby at the Hôtel des Rosiers in the old city. She went up to his room and he gave her an envelope containing a hundred thousand francs. She wiped away a tear, How can I thank you? —Another dinner, Bijou? I love your easy ways. And yet there's a shadow in your eyes. Am I wrong? She didn't answer. After dinner, they returned to the hotel. Toby asked, Can you guess what came next, Robinson? —No comment. —You've got it wrong, my friend. Our economics student showed up with an old book and read me a passage from it. You don't believe me, do you? She said, Mr Farmer, your reward is coming, and asked to go to the powder room. Five minutes later, she came back to the bedroom where I was sitting lost in thought in the only chair in the room. She was dressed in a long, worn peasant dress. And she said, This is my gift, Toby, words and images from another era, so that you understand that there has always been hope, even though the West has invariably mistreated us. I started to say that we weren't the only ones who'd been subjected to their misdeeds. Silence! she ordered, Listen! And she read to me from a book from another time, a book I had forgotten, Jean Ikellé Matiba's *Cette Afrique-là!* The story of Franz Mômha, a peasant in Cameroon at the beginning of the last century. Mômha and his family cutting furrows in the fields, tracing the lines of a new era in spite of the forced labour imposed by the German colonists. After her reading, the girl said, Fight, Toby, like Franz did! There will always be adversity, whether or not its face is that of an American company. We exist through resistance, Toby. That's our history. . . . The beautiful peasant sat down on my lap, straddling me, her scent of the sea enveloping me. She said, This reading wasn't just for show, Toby. I really wanted to read you those pages.

At the first glimmer of dawn, Toby said, continuing his story, the girl was no longer there between the sheets. Vanished. That was a year ago, Robinson. And I haven't seen her since. Disappeared, and her phone disconnected. The next day Ruth called me, beginning chapter two of our story. I don't know what became of Bijou. But the guy who just called said he had photos of my frolics with the pretend peasant girl. Said the girl is about to file a complaint because I supposedly forced her. Rape, that bastard said. Do you think The Firm entrapped me, Robinson? —I don't know. But it's clear she'd had her eye on you since your return from Savannah. You were spotted there with your activist friend. —Yes. But I won't go along with it. I'm not giving up. If they have photos that were supposedly taken while I was sleeping in her arms that night, well, they can go ahead and publish them! He shouted to Commissioner Shango, This is despicable, cowardly blackmail! Shameful! And you've reduced the chances of survival of the person I'm holding! —It's blackmail that can hurt you, Toby, I whispered. —I don't give a damn! I know what I did that night. And speaking of night, it will soon be sundown, Robinson. Will the night be my ally? Will it save you from the flames?

14

NIGHT, ROBINSON, NIGHT, AND RUTH, said Toby. He recounted an afternoon at Ruth's house on Habersham Street in the suburbs of Savannah. A bungalow, painted a fading, chalky blue, with a red door and shutters. The day before, Ruth had said, I want to show you something at my place, so make some excuse, a headache, indigestion, whatever, to avoid taking part in the outing, The Firm's smoke and mirrors of the day. I'll come and pick you up at your hotel about three, before the traffic gets bad, because I hate getting stuck on the road, breathing that foul air I avoid like the plague! . . . She arrived late, though, out of breath, saying, Sorry, I got held up at the hospital. There were some complicated cases today. . . . And while they were sitting in the traffic, she took her hand off the gearshift from time to time and reached over to squeeze Toby's arm. —I believe you're a very new cotton grower, she said, because your hands are much too soft and nice to have spent a thousand seasons tilling the soil, pulling up roots, and picking cotton. Could you be an imposter, or has some benevolent god preserved your hands from wear? And Toby answered that before plunging into the warm belly of the earth, his hands had for a long time done other work and roamed over other fields. —Over women's bodies, Toby? —Over books, actually, the pages and covers of books. —Were those pages and covers as pleasing to the touch as a lover's skin? —Almost. —Almost? Is there a difference then? —Yes. The temperature goes up faster on a lover's skin. —Ah, I see, I see.

They kept joking around like that to kill time while waiting in the traffic, until they reached the blue house an eternity later. The interior with its orange walls was neat and tidy; on counters and little tables there were pots overflowing with plants and flowers that seemed to be waiting for the mistress of the house to give them a drink, and for the sunshine that poured in as soon as she opened the curtains, with their patterns depicting old parchments and snippets of text from forgotten books. She watered her plants and Toby teased her, saying, If only humans could be treated as well as you treat your plants, Ruth! Then she made coffee for them in the kitchen, which Toby could see from where he was seated in the living room leafing through a magazine he'd found on the coffee table in front of the red sofa, pretending to be absorbed in reading while all he wanted was to fix his eyes on the luminous, often blushing face of the splendid redhead in her flowered shirt and tight-fitting pants. At one point while the coffeemaker was releasing its drops of arabica, he looked up from his magazine and surprised her peeking at him. On being discovered, she reacted like a thief caught red-handed, spinning around to a cupboard, saying, So, the sugar, where did I put it?

Sitting in the living room, their bodies almost touching, they drank the coffee in silence, self-conscious, two college students on their first date, which bothered Toby, because as far back as he could remember, he had never lost his cool in such situations. —Come with me, Ruth said when they had emptied their cups, and Toby followed her to a door across from the little eating area between the kitchen and living room, a door that opened onto a narrow old wooden staircase to the basement. The basement was a strange world, a cavern from another time, with a great many things shut away as if to protect them from the destructive world outside. In a corner was an old fireplace and there were shelves screwed to the brick walls painted a matte gray. On the shelves and on two long tables against the walls were displayed various pieces, a collection of things from the past—postcards with serrated edges, heavy scissors of rusted metal, keys, embroidered placemats, a harmonica that had once sung the blues of the South, a

Bible, a silver chalice that looked like it needed polishing, coins, and some leatherbound books, about which Ruth said, Unfortunately those are copies or reprints. Old stuff is my hobby, and here's one that's the real thing, if I can believe a collector I showed it to. It's a first edition of Thoreau's *Walden*. Published in Boston in 1854 by Ticknor and Fields. Have you read it? —Yes, Ruth. I did my degree in English way back when. That's a very nice item. The brown leather binding feels warm, as if it retained the heat of all the hands that have touched it. And those traces of grease and the scratches are all from those people's lives. —What do you think of Thoreau's writing? —I think that, being alone, he was able to find in nature and deep within himself a life that was more intense, richer, and more meaningful than the plans for progress devised in our cities. However, to fight against the slave-holding system of government he loathed, he had to come out of his seclusion. Maybe the lesson is that living on the margins of society, by choice or of necessity, prepares one to come back to the centre to act. —So the centre is inescapable? —I think so, Ruth. —It seems to me he understood the place in the world where one has to be. —His hermit's cabin at Walden Pond? She laughed and handed me another book by Thoreau, saying, This one, *Civil Disobedience*, is unfortunately not a first edition. The need for resistance, Toby. And there's no resistance without action. . . . They sat on a thick white carpet in front of the fireplace, Ruth holding Toby's free hand.

Toby spoke to me of the warmth of her skin. A fire fuelled by her anger at the world or by something deeper that was burning inside her? After they made love, Ruth, had cried on his chest, and Winnie standing dry-eyed, her head bowed over the dead body of Samuel Brown, had said to herself that this was no longer a body for love, no longer the hands and the belly and the warm breath on her body, her breasts and her sex, which during the torture of Samuel had shrivelled, and Pastor Bill touching her shoulder had repeated, The ways of God . . . and Toby, the lighter in his fist, said, I'll have your skin, Robinson. —You won't do that, you aren't that stupid! I shouted. The little flame was dancing five centimetres from my arm. Ed roared, Toby, if you touch a single hair on your hostage's head, you won't get anything! —Your inaction distresses me, Toby replied. And I'm warning you, with your next attempt at blackmail, everything will go up in smoke! —Toby, the idea of sending a mission to the savannahs to assess your losses and your needs deserves to be considered, the Minister of Agriculture gave us his assurances. —Bullshit, nothing but bullshit! I don't believe it! We don't want anything but our two hundred million in reparations! And I've waited long enough!

13

5:03 PM. TOBY MURMURED, It looks like you're right, Robinson. We're completely alone. —Yes, Toby, you're an orphan, crazy and lost, which is why you've no choice but to tell your story, to bring back the past and formulate hypotheses of future mornings and drunken times outside these walls where we're holed up, in order to give yourself the illusion of existing and convince yourself that you aren't on a desert island. Alone, defeated, and dead, Friday. But with the meagre consolation that your bones, white and clean and immaculate like the relics of saints or extinct species, will be exhibited in the great Museum of the Vanquished that will be visited by the descendants of the victors, armed with smiles, foolish surprise, and cameras, photographing what's left of you. Yes, you're screwed! —Nice sermon, Robinson, Toby laughed, and said he didn't envision his passing to posterity in the terrifying white solitude of a skeleton exhibited in a futuristic gallery of the vanquished of history. And besides, he said, you're very naïve. The vanquished won't even have that museum to consecrate their remains, it would be too embarrassing for the victors, unless a new breed of madmen decides to bring the losers out of obscurity. No, I don't want to be a useless relic, Robinson. Life, our potential passions and pleasures, is here and now! And what if I told you that Ruth wants a child? Yes, she wants to produce a creature of the future with my humble self. —Congratulations! —It's just an idea, Robinson. —Seriously, Toby, you're done for. But meanwhile, you're struggling in your miserable skin. —Shut up, Robinson! At least, I'm doing something! —You know what, Toby, I said, the only living things nothing can touch anymore are creatures of oil, gouache, or charcoal. Like the ones in Bruegel's painting. Because we're still the vanquished, and I've been chasing after the secret of their victory since I was twenty, since my first visit to Vienna. And I was there again three months ago, trying to understand that absurd joy painted on a piece of wood, to understand why at the back of the scene, in the middle of the revelry, a fellow is trying to draw away a shy miss who is resisting him. To understand what was supporting the arms and the spirits of the people in Thomas Hart Benton's *Cotton Pickers*, which I saw at the Art Institute of Chicago a few months earlier. To understand, after seeing the gesture of giving in that painting where the woman in the white blouse and ochre skirt is offering a drink of water to a kneeling companion crushed by fatigue, who appears in great need of it. The painting is said to have been inspired by a journey Benton made to Georgia in the 1920s, the America of the post-Civil War era, a time when the more prosperous white owners leased land to the poor Blacks to farm in return for a share of their harvest. Seeing the straw hats worn by the harvesters bent over the plants, it's easy to imagine how intense the heat must have been; obviously, it wasn't yet a time of merrymaking for those people, history tells us that sharecropping was to their disadvantage, and yet in Benton's painting I perceived neither anger nor grievance, only the constancy of the movement, like that of a rower or a swimmer; to swim, to move, to harvest, so as not to collapse under the uncaring blue sky. That, I managed to understand. Like Winnie: to hold on, not to crumple. But she recovered a little energy because it occurred to her more and more that she too could try—as Samuel once had—to make holes in the great work, to weaken it, to destroy it bit by bit, and that was why she now went to the fields with a knife hidden under her dress. No, she would not just make gentle little cuts in the belly of the great work with her blade. Yes, like Winnie, to understand also that it's not enough merely to remain standing.

TO UNDERSTAND TOO THAT THERE WAS JOY on Grandmother's face in that painting by her German man that I only saw later on, it must have been hidden I didn't know where. Grandmother had said, And yet, it's not bad at all, to me it's your grandfather's most successful one, his best. It was an oil, quite modest in size, eighty by fifty centimetres and as soon as I saw it, I had a feeling I'd seen it before, it was familiar to me, even though I was sure it was the first time I was seeing it. I was twenty then and the painting dated from the mid-1970s, but it seemed like the present, scenes from life repeated for generations on our plateaus, reinforcing the feeling that I'd always known them. The work was titled *Ablo, an Afternoon Wedding*.

Ablo was the village square, encircled by impressive kapok, mango, breadfruit, and flame trees that towered over old bamboo benches where villagers were sitting after returning from the fields. Some were filling their pipes, others were already blowing smoke towards the tops of the sapota trees, still others were downing palm wine, competing with the flies hanging onto the edges of the gourds they brought to their lips, while two drummers, their tam-tams clutched between their thighs, celebrated the characters standing across from them in the middle of the square. The village chief was identifiable from the kente-cloth wrapper around his waist and the cloth thrown over one shoulder as well as his black velvet headwear dotted with gold buttons. He was talking with the two other people in the painting, a woman and a man who were presumably a couple, seeing the way they were standing side by side very close to keep from being separated by an evil spirit from the peak at Kebo. The peak dominated the whole scene. The man, also in kente, was white, and the woman could only be Grandmother, her bare arm pressed against that of her German man. Grandmother had commented on the scene, It was the afternoon of our wedding, the whole village celebrated in our honour in Ablo. Your grandfather was shy, but I was proud, I was the daughter of nobody, who through this marriage was taking my revenge on destiny.

I also recognized the scene because it was based on a black-and-white photo dating from a day in June 1949. The first picture in the family album, which also contained portraits of my parents in their carefree youth. To paint that picture, Grandfather had imagined or invented colours that were nonexistent in the black-and-white photo, and I felt he was successful in that. Colours revealed by his genius and his visceral attachment to our part of Africa from the first day he set foot on its red earth in his missionary's garb. Grandmother said, What your grandfather painted is less our plateaus and their people than the love he felt for them. . . . And I realized that oil painting of a wedding celebration that Grandfather had kept hidden at the bottom of a trunk was, like a work by a Bruegel or a Giorgione, simply the expression of the tumultuous age-old relationship of man and nature.

A FAINT ODOUR OF ROTTEN EGGS began to fill the room. Was it coming from outside or from the air vents above our heads? Toby pinched his nose and said sadly that he was thinking of his parents and of Monsieur Antonin, who towards the end of his life stopped trimming his beard, which gave him, a man who had spent his life in possession of things, a strangely austere appearance, and of his twin daughters, who had returned to France before they were fifteen and who had been carefully shielded from what their father called Negro stupidity and depravity. Toby was thinking of all those people, but most of all of the fields. Because, he said, I come from there, Robinson. I remember my parents' fields in the good years of the farm, the late 1980s, when, with the master dead, my father supervised things and shared the profits equally with the widow, after the Auvergne people had left their house, which was falling into ruin in the middle of the fields—it must be said that it dated from the beginning of the last century, but the problem was that it had been poorly maintained—my father walking through the fields and touching the plants, Levant cotton, the variety with the finest fibres. And I can see my mother walking with him, annoyed because he was dawdling, going from one plant to the next; after all, they were only the same cotton plants that, each season, turned the whole area green all the way to the hot horizon, covering it with a cloak of promise, because, for sure, the harvest would be good, my mother furious, not understanding why her pigheaded husband insisted on her being beside him on his walks through the fields among the harvesters, who were resting after a whole morning spent picking the cotton, labour dating from ancient times, from when the first boll burst open five thousand years ago in a valley in India. Those men and women my father referred to by the strange term "men with cotton hands" or "cotton men," who spent weeks harvesting, ginning, and packing the cotton into big baskets made of raffia and palm leaves, men who had finally merged with the vegetable matter to form a single body with cotton hands and movements, and it was no longer the land that grew the cotton, it was the hands, the peasants opened their hard, calloused palms and the round white mass of cotton appeared, luminous. It was another time, Robinson. Or at least the beautiful story of another time, because I know you'll tell me every golden age also has its ugliness! But I'm talking about the movie that played in front of my child's eyes every season; anyway, at the time, we didn't talk about the livestock that was poisoned, decimated, nor the waterways being turned into liquid yellow death, nor the mutant fruits swollen with the helium of science, unrecognizable in colour or flavour.

And I don't remember anymore in what book of history or biology, I, a curious, inquisitive child, one day came across that image I immediately copied, which I remember showing to my father, impatient to see his reaction, while he was standing deep in conversation with the labourers, I remember he finally turned to me and I lifted my small square of white paper up to his eyes, blocking his view of the rest of the landscape of men, plants, and animals. A drawing. I had traced a photograph of an old woodcut in a book, a woodcut dating from the fifteenth century, an image of a strange shrub, apparently a cotton plant, whose fruits, the dry open bolls, revealed, not the hoped-for fibre, but rather heads of sheep. "Wool tree," read the caption, the cotton seen as a wool more sumptuous than that produced by sheep. And the sheep, in pens or tied to stakes at the edge of the fields, must not have looked favourably on the scene, knowing very well that for my father the vegetable fibre counted for much more than theirs, grubby and soiled with mud. The sheep bleated their anger, while in the harvesters' hands the pure wool burst open, soon to be transported in bales to the distant lands of Europe and America, while in his madness old Corporal Yambo continued to make his bags of soil under my mother's sad gaze. And I have to go through with it, Robinson, for Yambo and all those people, said Toby, otherwise those guys outside won't lift a finger to compensate us! . . . And the lighter reappeared in his fingers, the little flame, and to make us take him seriously, he would do it. —No Toby! And Ed, alert to the slightest sound coming from the room, shouted, Toby, at this very moment the final details of a proposal to you are being discussed. So don't do anything you may regret later. And we have to go forward with this exhibition. Donors will come to it who are prepared to help our growers. What a waste if it all fell through! —Bullshit, boss. A load of crap! I didn't ask for promises, I asked for two hundred million. And I repeat, one more attempt at blackmail, and you'll have asked for it, boss! I'd like to see the look on your face when you see your friend's dead body!

10

5:14 PM. THE DEAD BODY OF SAMUEL BROWN lies at the base of the pillory in the middle of the fields, the overseer's dogs have calmed down, and a paper bird has alighted on the floor between Toby and my outstretched legs. A letter. —What news does the bird bring, Toby? —I don't know, Robinson, and I'm not interested! I don't trust that paper. It's another dirty blackmail attempt or a trap. I could open it, and boom, we'd be blown away like so much dust! I don't trust the bird and what it has in its belly. —It's a very thin envelope. —That doesn't matter. They might have put a powder inside that'll blind me when I open it. —I don't think so. And even if you were blinded, you'd still be able to wreak havoc as you promised, wouldn't you? You'd still be able to light a fire. —So then a poison, Robinson. I sniff the envelope and I drop dead. —That would be a murder, and I could talk. They wouldn't take such a risk. —So you'd talk if those bastards put a bullet in me? —I'd answer the questions I was asked. —Bullshit! I'm still very much alive, Robinson. —Yes, alive. For now. —Well, well. So then, I'll open that envelope, since you'll talk if it happens that I'm pulverized in front of your eyes. —I'm not promising anything. Shango interrupted us, Toby, you're not sure you want to find out what's in the envelope? It's not a trap. This is your last chance, Toby!

Toby nervously tore open the envelope and pulled out a sheet of paper. Apparently there was no deadly powder or perfume in the belly of the bird. Those scumbags! he said, reading the letter, his face expressionless. Unable to contain my impatience, I asked, So, Toby? —So,

Robinson, The Firm has a lot of nerve. —Explain. —Just listen to what the bird has delivered. *Dear sir, for several hours we have been following your actions, which in our opinion are anything but constructive. We continue to assert that with our modified seeds and herbicides, provided at very low prices to the growers of this country, agricultural production, especially of cotton, has been substantially improved. And to mark this milestone in the country's development, we have partially financed the construction of the Museum of the Green Revolution. The purpose: to pay homage to the brave workers of the land of this country who provide for thousands of families. We are not the wolves you think we are. It is not in your interest nor in the interest of cooperation between The Firm and the government of this country for you to continue your regrettable action. We will not be able to accede to your demands, which are based on groundless allegations. However, if you cease your action, we will be disposed to undertake discussions with you. I will have an honest proposal to make to you.* The letter was signed by a certain Peter Baye, assistant to the local representative of The Firm.

Toby came back and sat down against the wall across from me. Was I still mad at him while the pain returned to my joints? Commissioner Shango's voice betrayed his impatience, So are you coming out of there to talk with the people in charge, Toby? —It's a fuck-up, Shango! I'm not going along. You can go ahead and snipe at us. Or are you afraid this brand-new building constructed at the expense of the taxpayers and The Firm will be destroyed? That's it, you've been given your instructions, do everything possible to save this place and avoid a disturbance a few days from an official visit that's very important to our goddamn government. Who's coming anyway? The prime minister of China or of India? And what juicy contracts will be signed? Robinson, what is my skin worth? In the past few hours its price has undergone extraordinary inflation? —Your skin doesn't count, Friday. —Don't call me that! —In the story, you're still Friday, the native, the peasant, the . . . —My name is Toby Kunta! But you, who are you?

9

THE ROTTEN SMELL WAS GETTING STRONGER. Toby swore, For sure they've put something in the ventilation ducts. To drive me out, Robinson. But it can't be lethal, since you're here. So I owe you one. Oh, if you hadn't been here! But I'm not going to give in just because it stinks a bit in this room, huh? That would be dumb. When I was in Georgia, I said to myself that it would be dumb not to see more of Savannah while I was there. So two or three times, at Ruth's suggestion, I made the excuse of a persistent headache so as not to take part in the performances put on by The Firm.

And while the other growers in his group were being subjected to The Firm's lessons on things transgenic, Toby went out walking with the redhead, encountering the inevitable tourists gobbling up their raspberry ice cream, an old lady picking up her mutt's pretty little brown turds with surgical precision, and a person who asked them the way to the Boone Hall Plantation, and when Ruth opened her mouth to answer, someone behind them thundered, We're not in Charleston here! Let's get serious, forget Major Boone's azaleas, oaks, and magnolias! It's only tourists who wear out their eyes admiring our vegetation! Me, I'm off to go visit my buddy Jack who got a good few years in the Coastal State Prison. . . . They turned around; the man, who was drinking from a bottle of whisky, was walking away, his silhouette like that of a starving galley slave, staggering between the green of the oak trees above and the red of the cobblestones.

They continued on to the old town, walking in silence, not wanting to risk disturbing the moment they were experiencing—or hurrying to savour that moment before it was disturbed, as things around us and within us are naturally disturbed—towards the wharfs of the Savannah River, passing by, after Bay Street, the metal footbridges of Factors Walk with their flaking paint. Toby continued, As we walked on the ballast stones of the streets, Ruth told me I had taken a huge risk with the Bt cotton. In the harbour a paddleboat was anchored, the *Georgia Queen*, preparing to transport other eager visitors towards their weird dreams. We sat down on a bench looking out on the lapping water. Beside her, I was a shy, awkward boy again.

I'm sad because I'm aching for Ruth, I have to touch her or I'll die, Toby continued. The next night, we hung out in the bars, the ideal place to take the city's pulse. We found ourselves in a warm lair of a pub with dark brick walls, lost amid the rumblings of loud voices, the clinking of glasses, arguments, laughter, and country music sung off-key by a one-eyed man perched on a stool with his guitar. Afterwards, we prowled around in the squares where the sad, lonely ghosts of the American Old South still linger. But instead of an ephemeral being slipping through the trees, we encountered a young woman all flesh and smiles, who, without a glance at Ruth, asked me if I wanted company. —So am I invisible? Ruth asked. Scram! She was almost trembling, Robinson. She must love me, right, as ugly, antiquated, and imperfect as I am. Plus, these past five years have driven me crazy. So I'll definitely have to burn you. Sorry, my friend. . . . The little flame moved steadily closer, I squeezed my lips together, already feeling the burning, and tried to pull my arm back, but I was cornered, it was no use, I screamed, Stop fooling around, Toby! It hurts! —Careful, Toby! Shango roared. And Ed Kaba shouted, Toby, we'll soon have something else for you, so don't torture your hostage! —What do you mean, soon? There was nothing concrete in the letter from your guy from The Firm! It was just insulting! So get ready to say goodbye to your buddy.

8

5:32 PM. TOBY STARTED PACING back and forth again. From the walls, the peasants' faces stared pensively at him, incredulous, almost mocking. Those men and women on matte or glossy paper were unconcerned by our misfortune; worse, they laughed at it, and because they would remain cold photographs for all eternity, they would continue to make fun of us, their laughter and derision following us in an endless loop of time between the walls of the exhibition hall, time now made up of the smell of kerosene and burnt paper, our incandescent breath, the silence of the walls, the cold floor under our butts, the aura of remains and rubbish of the items exhibited by my jailer, the distant quality of the nocturnal memories and epics he spoke of, echoes, fire, and shouts from outside that hardly shook the walls, the dead time barely interrupted since the twelve strokes of noon by the static on the transistor radio, like the moaning of a capricious kid, this time seemed in no way to have decided to yield its privileges as a god endowed with all powers but whose one plan was to ignore us, there at the heart of misfortune. And it seemed to me now that I understood Toby's actions. Besides the fact that he no longer knew who to turn to, that he was desperate, destroying these things that created the prison of dead time, burning them, was an attempt to escape, or at least to cheat the cold continuity of emptiness and nothingness through the madness of his action. Also, to get out of this production by a wise guy with a camera in which the peasants had been placed like puppets in a fake countryside, those awkward women and men amid the cotton bolls and baskets of fruits and tubers. It was perhaps not The Firm that Toby was angry with, but actually with his people of the land who were susceptible to all kinds of manipulation, subject as most of them were to that fraudulent god sent to them by The Firm as the materialization of his promise of salvation, of supreme happiness.

Looking me in the eye, Toby said that Ruth was in bad shape, depressed, They stole all the things she had collected, Robinson, all those beautiful old things she showed me in her basement. The sudden loss of so many of her mementos was devastating. She hasn't gotten over it. She suspects a guy from her neighbourhood, a junkie who was often short of cash for his fix of heroine. She did consult someone, one of those so-called experts. But it didn't do any good, plus the guy's services were ridiculously expensive. She can't work anymore and she's flat broke. I've got to help her. To get treatment in a good clinic and plan for the future. I have to send her what she needs. Money. She hasn't asked me for anything, and she's sure to refuse at first. She really loved that book. She feels that Thoreau was one of the first to have a responsible attitude to this old Earth. I've got to give her a hand, Robinson or she won't make it. And then she'll be able to buy herself another first edition of the book if she finds one.

You know what, Toby? I said after a long silence. I was right. Your whole campaign is for Ruth, not to defend the growers. Basically, you don't give a damn about your buddies in the savannahs, the sick kids, the exterminated livestock, the suicides, or the people who are dying. —You're insulting me, Robinson. —No, I'm making an observation. You've created all this uproar to try to save your glorious redhead. —That's not true! —It is so! —What do you think I am? —Would you have dragged us into all this if your Ruth hadn't been in trouble? —I think so. —You do? —You're insulting me! There has to be that essential element that pushes a person to take action, right? In my case, I admit it, it's Ruth, I can't deny it. —Aren't your grower friends essential? —Yes they are. But I don't have to justify myself, Robinson. Since when does a hostage have the right to demand explanations from the person holding him?

Wali's hanging and Ruth's troubles made me decide to take action. Maybe I wouldn't have done anything on behalf of anyone if she didn't exist. Maybe I just would have moped around in my corner and gone occasionally with a few of the others vanquished by The Firm to protest feebly at their offices. It was for Ruth that I decided to no longer be one of the vanquished. —You're a poor soldier in a futile campaign. Once Ruth is back on her feet, what will you do? You'll return to your lethargy? —I'm no wimp, Robinson! And who are you to judge me? I don't know squat about you. You're a journalist, you said? You've covered the suicides of the peasants in Rajasthan, and what else? My name is Toby Kunta. What name do you answer to? —Is this an interrogation? —You know quite a bit about me, Robinson. Who are *you*? —I speak when I want to. —Who are you? What are you afraid of? Could you be an imposter? —What does it matter if my name is Alpha or Omega? Actually, Robinson suits me. —Come on, tell me! —Ouyi. my name is Ouyi Hoffer. —Hoffer? —My grandfather was German. —Interesting. That explains it. —How so? —Your face, your skin, I was thinking. —There's nothing special about my face! —It's not your face but your history that's of interest to me. What was his occupation, your forebear from Prussia? —So, I see the interrogation is continuing. —I need to get to know you a little. And maybe I'll decide that your life is worth sparing. Which I doubt, however. —He was a pastor and a painter. —Nice combination. And I suppose your grandmother was a chaste churchgoer who fell in love with her pastor after a private reading of some psalms? —Screw you! —And your parents? —Dead. —You must have family around Bremen. —Why Bremen? —Weren't the first German missionaries who came to the west coast of this continent from there? —You're very astute. —I'll take the compliment. So do you have relatives on the Old Continent? —I've found traces of a few, yes. —And do you see them? —No, I don't. I'm beat, Toby. —Yes, you look uncomfortable. —We're in a black hole, Toby. —Yes. A nice hole, and we're both looking for the same worn-out sun.

7

NOW WE WERE ENVELOPED BY THE SMELL, a mixture of sewer gas and rotten eggs. Maybe it wouldn't suffocate us, but it was barely tolerable. I tried to bring back memories of other smells, like the perfume of a former lover, while Toby repeated, I have to help Ruth. Robinson, are you listening to me? I was hearing other voices, murmurings of ghosts, my grandmother telling of her love for her German man and his mischief, I was touching letters and photos that had survived from the past on the plateaus, seeing in front of my eyes the house clinging to a hillside before the erosion ended up toppling it into the brambles, the dandelions, the red rock, and lower still onto the two graves being gradually swallowed up by the earth and rock dust that came down from the heights to erase all traces of anything on the ground. And because the peasants little by little had left the area and migrated to the big city, it seemed that no one passed the graves of Fania Tepe and Hans Hoffer anymore, no one to pull up the weeds around the flagstones as they went by, to pick up the two fallen terracotta pots that had once held a few flowers and put them back in place, no one, just rats and a few indifferent lizards who had taken up residence on the flagstones and furnished their quarters with relics from the grandparents as well as whatever the little creatures brought back from their expeditions on the roads and in the yards of houses.

I almost never mention my grandparents anymore, or I simply have no occasion to, since the month of June ten years ago, when I came back to be with my grandmother, who was sick, in the final days of her life.

Telling Toby that story would be giving something to him and he would try to connect me to some vague lineage, land, origin, or identity card. Hasn't he recognized the strangeness of my half-breed face, the fact that I could be from anywhere and everywhere, and so could only be a missionary-adventurer as my grandfather was, an adventurer and a colonist, the label stuck on him by history, although, as Grandmother said, from the first day he arrived on our plateaus, Hans Hoffer wanted to talk like us, to possess our speech, our songs and rhythms, and the day he got here, he stopped being a foreigner, singing loud and clear in Ewe the Biblical hymns—translated by the first missionaries from Bremen—during services and evening gatherings. Your grandfather possessed the language of this place, he is of this place, Grandmother said to me. And I, his grandson, did not want to be seen as an outsider either, a hapless pedlar of miracles and tall tales, like those agents, lobbyists, and ambassadors of The Firm who crisscrossed the world selling their biotechnology, but I was neither a peasant of our plateaus or savannahs nor a town-dweller of our tropics; since Grandmother's death all my connections were broken. And Toby, reading my troubled face, said, You're not credible, Robinson. In order to be, you would have to reconnect to something, better yet to people, preferably living ones. Therefore I'm right to accuse you of not knowing what's going on, you landed here from a world that has nothing to do with mine. I've flushed you out, your lineage is that of those insatiable prospectors, investors, exploiters, profiteers who, from mine to mine, from drill site to drill site, from experimenting to marketing of miracle cures for soils and bodies, always call the shots. So you don't deserve to be spared by me.

Toby had gotten it right, and if for a decade I'd gone from country to country to meet the workers of the land, it was only to erase from myself the imprint of those people of my Germanic lineage whose traces I had found, cousins of Grandfather Hans who made their fortunes from prospecting and mines in Cameroon and Rhodesia. I would arrive in the Indian state of Bihar, in the countryside of Guatemala or Punjab, in the province of Gourma in Burkina Faso, and I would listen to the peasants telling their stories, I'd take notes, record, photograph, and eventually turn out some nice articles that most people would never read. All that without feeling the fear they felt. That horrible emptiness followed by knife stabs in the stomach, that feeling those growers had learned to live with was foreign to me until now, until the minute when Toby started the fire of his action. For the first time, I was facing the fire. Toby had given me the gift of this fear, this fear of living as the price to be paid for being able to say I am one of them. To say I am of those fields that I left at the age of twelve to go to school, entrusted by Grandmother to one of her brothers, Uncle Okelo, who lived down there in Le Port. And maybe things would have been different if it hadn't been for that exodus from the capital that took me to the doors of university with my German passport, far from the country and from those fields that Grandmother had never wanted to leave, even when, fifteen years ago, her German man had made his final exit.

I continued, I could have been not so different, Toby, I could have said, as my ex, Oumi, did, that I was just like anyone else. Oumi, a fiery gaze and a rage, there where it all began ten years ago. And if I came back to this country, it was also to make a fresh start. Oumi, a ravishing and sorrowful Uzbek from the Fergana Valley. And if I've displayed a kind of distance between myself and the people of the land since the beginning of Toby's action, it was to try to forget my Oumi, who I met when I was covering a story in Tashkent. Oumi was doing an investigation of child labour, I should say child slavery, and had agreed to replace my interpreter and guide, who had to leave to deal with a family emergency. To try to forget Oumi and all those people she reminded me of. People with bodies broken one September morning on that cotton that absolutely had to be gathered by hand to preserve the beauty, the purity of the fibre, above all to not do as the Americans did, who harvested the cotton using combines, with all the dirt and dead plants. That day in September 2005, we were in Jizzakh in a field that extended as far as the eye could see. Translating an unhappy harvest worker, Oumi said angrily, By hand! The cotton has to be beautiful. The men, women, and children are forced labour, no one gives a damn about their health! And also, with the amount of water it takes to grow the plants, they've almost completely dried up the Aral Sea! The cotton isn't a source of pride, it's a national disgrace! That's how Oumi spoke, her heart filled with rage and impotence. Impotence because, an expatriate in Germany for several years, she was far from Fergana and couldn't do anything to alter the tragedy. Because you had to be there in the country, to disturb them, to get to those apparatchiks in their cool offices in Tashkent who sent the people to toil outdoors. That was how she raged, my lover.

Oumi liked to go with me on my trips when she could. In 2010, after a week investigating the spinning mills in Dacca, in Bangladesh, we went to Gujarat, in India, where the peasants had begun to abandon organic cotton for BCI cotton, the fabulous Better Cotton Initiative created in 2009, a fraudulent invention, another load of shit, cotton that was supposed to be produced with very little pesticides or water, and Oumi's question was, What does that mean, very little, does its production respect nature or not? She was enraged, but the peasants demonstrated, with supporting evidence, that they were earning a better living with the less demanding BCI cotton. What about the environment? she repeated. But she knew, nature and the environment don't mean much when you have a lot of mouths to feed. And then there was the treachery, the cynicism of the spinning mills that passed off genetically modified cotton as BCI. Oumi's talk of clean green nature in those remote areas of western India was an indulgence, the whim of a spoiled child from the West. But I remembered an afternoon when Oumi found her smile again. We were visiting the farm of Indira Maheshwari, a good woman who proudly showed us her organic cotton produced without chemical fertilizers or pesticides, kala cotton, a variety said to be surprisingly resistant to drought and thus require little water. Experts call it a robust *G. herbaceum*. Oumi was ecstatic, but I wondered how long Indira Maheshwari and the last diehards of organic cotton would be able to resist the invasion of BCI. And in the Kutch region, we visited the Khamir Centre, where women with miraculous hands, angels determined to stop the extinction of hope, magical artisans and dyers were making magnificent fabrics with kala cotton. Oumi, I recalled, wrapped a blue and scarlet turban in Ajrakh patterns, splendid arabesques, around her neck. The peasants and artisans we met gave us the gift of all that beauty. And we understood that there was only one word, a single word, to define their action: resistance.

Oumi. Two months ago, we lived the final chapter of our story. She had decided to go back to live in Uzbekistan, close to her people, she said. She hadn't dared to ask me what I would do there if I decided to follow her. In Berlin we had our work and our routines. But I told her, There you'll have to find your bearings, the country is foreign to you now. I should have kept my mouth shut. Her anger rose like a mad wave and she retorted, Those are my roots! But I understand, you don't have roots anymore! I want to be there to fight for the kids, to fight tooth and nail. And you should do the same, get involved, go further than reports and articles, join the struggle. . . . Was she trying to hurt me in order to give our break-up an ultimate reason? It was true that I had no roots or anchors anymore, my grandparents and parents were rotting in the earth of the tropics. However, I no longer recognized the woman who had once said of the two of us that our roots were the road and the wind and the sky of the countries we visited together. On the last night of our seven years of living together—after three summers of seeing each other—she had espoused a discourse of the native land and roots that I felt was outdated. With Oumi gone, I wanted to forget the land and roots and my sad concerns, Samuel Brown, who left me only to return the next morning with his skin empty, in the earth. But now Toby's questions were bringing back ghosts and memories.

6

TOBY BROUGHT ME BACK TO THAT DAY in 1980 when, as Grandmother told me, They called the church. Your grandfather had a meeting there with the parish committee. It was only there that we had a telephone. It was a dark day, my boy, when we lost our Bayo. He and Mayim, your mother, were going to work in the capital when their car was struck by a truck. When your grandfather was told, he collapsed on the ground. Luckily he wasn't alone. A part of us was amputated, I just wanted to die, but there was you. You were two years old, you were at home with the woman who took care of you when the tragedy occurred. Your mother's family wanted the poor couple to be buried in the capital in the cemetery at the beach, near the streets and squares of the old city where the two had met four years earlier. You came here to us after the funeral. The in-laws weren't opposed. I must say they had less to be pitied for than we did, your mother had six brothers and sisters who could give each other support. For us, if you hadn't been there, life would have been a desert, emptiness—your grandfather even considered abandoning his mission and going back to Bremen. If it's any consolation to you, I too never knew my parents. My father died in the trenches in the Great War, in a place with the strange name of Ovillers-la-Boisselle, I was told. When my mother died, I was raised by the first pastor of the Evangelical Presbyterian Church in a little village in the mountains. He's the one your grandfather replaced. My godfather sent me to train as a nurse in the capital. I had come back to visit him when he was leaving to return to Germany, and that was when I met his replacement, your grandfather.

Grandmother dabbed her teary eyes and continued, Your father worked at the Gulf Railway Company. He took care of the machines, but what he really wanted to be was a chemist. And for that, he would have had to go to Europe. But God does as he pleases. As for your mother, she taught at Marius Moutet primary school, in the oldest quarter of Le Port. You can imagine the tears her unhappy students shed when she passed away. They were two wonderful young people. Your father had a sense of what is essential in life. Although he had moved to the capital, he came to see us every Saturday. And here you are, my child, you've been a country boy for ten years now. I remember, a few months after the tragedy, your grandfather said, We're in a fairy tale from the Brothers Grimm, my dear Fania, we are the poor, childless country people to whom fate one day gave a little boy in the story "Daumesdick," or "Tom Thumb," one of the tales that were told to us in Lower Saxony. So let's try to make a man of our Daumesdick. And Grandmother added, During your first four years here, he called you Daumesdick, ignoring my indignation. Daumesdick, careful, you'll tumble into that ravine! Daumesdick, could you hand me my shoes? Daumesdick, those snakes, as small as they are, are not toys! And I was afraid you would remain the size of a thumb like the child in the story! I was afraid of losing you in the acacia thickets and dead leaves! But God heard my prayers and you grew very tall, and I believe you're going to surpass your poor father's height.

I continued, So I would not remain the ridiculously little and fragile Tom Thumb of the tale, I would acquire a tough skin and a presence in the world, a kind of substance, but I wondered what would happen when the voices of Grandmother and Grandfather went silent, when their skins ended up feeding the red clay of our plateaus, in what circles of sounds, bodies, and lives would I attain that solidity and that presence? This was the question that was bugging me before I discovered the painting by Bruegel, and now it seemed that my questions and my quest would end here, with Toby, who was again approaching my arm with his lighter, and an unbearable pain shot through my back, Oww! Ed immediately reacted, Toby, stop, I'm told there's something concrete, that someone is going to call you any minute now. — Oh, yeah? Hurry up then or else you won't have a chance to speak to your friend one last time! And just so you understand once and for all that I'm not bluffing, I'm cutting half of these horrible photographs into little pieces! And Winnie knew that it was a matter of cutting holes with the knife in the belly of the great work, holes of rebellion but also a place of one's own, a life and dreams, especially the dream of seeing her little Abraham go to school and become—maybe, she wasn't sure—a skin that counted.

5

THE STENCH OF PUTREFACTION coming through the air ducts seemed
to be lessening, or else the smells of childhood had settled in my head,
casting into oblivion the present, which stank of cesspool, tragedy, and
failure, while Toby, having checked the clock and seen that it was 6
PM, shifted into high gear and violently removed more images from
the walls. He continued his diligent work of destruction, breaking the
frames and tearing out the photographs, until there were a dozen of
them reduced to a jumble of wood and paper on the floor, and each
time he finished one off, he seemed to be turning a page, moving a
step further away from the grower he had been for the past five years.
With nervous hands he demolished a photograph of women piling
cotton into big raffia baskets and one of a worker full of faith carrying a big drum of liquid on his back and spraying it on his fields with
a wand, and he exclaimed, That's what I do with your damn glyphosate! And another one, of a truck overflowing with the fibre, a white
mound whose impressive mass dominated the surrounding scene of
ripe fields, bodies bent over the cotton bolls, and an indifferent sky.
Toby was destroying everything that connected him to the land and
the cotton, but I sensed in his actions a kind of heartbreak, and an
impossibility. Cotton was his history.

After setting the photographs on fire and throwing them into the
street, he went back to his bag in the middle of the exhibition hall,
took out two things I had no trouble identifying although they were
strange: a section of a log, the wood bleached by time and weather,

and a rock the size of two clasped hands, also polished by the seasons. I said to myself that they must be treasures he had taken from the belly of the earth. He placed them carefully on display stands, stepped back a few paces to assess the effect, looked satisfied, and returned to sit down across from my corner. He explained, The rock and the piece of wood are for Kali the widow and her kids, one-eyed Kali and her brood. She lost all her livestock, poisoned by the spring behind her patch of land, and found herself with nothing to feed her offspring, six mouths open to the wind and the emptiness of the savannahs. The family lived as best it could on bitter roots and leaves, and also by stealing from neighbouring fields, but hunger ate a bigger and bigger hole in their bellies, hunger shrunk their silhouettes, now skeletal except for the bellies swollen with worms. And in the evenings of the days without bread—Robinson, that reminds me of a horrible story my mother used to tell—one-eyed Kali would put a rock under the embers in the stove in front of her hut. She would say to the famished kids gathered in a gloomy group around the fire that it was meat, agouti, good bushmeat, that they had to be patient until it was cooked, patient until the end of the night plagued by the voracious insects devouring their skin. But it seemed that the odourless meat was extremely tough, the fire trying in vain to render it edible, the fire crackling until the end of the night, until the little eyes watching the miraculous dish cooking were exhausted and the kids, finally overcome by sleep or the holes in their bellies, slumped to the ground at the foot of the stove that one-eyed Kali continued to feed with wood, seeking to push the limits of the miracle. And the next day the scene would be played out again, this time Kali promising the children good tasty fish, a piece of wood buried under the embers. But occasionally a neighbour would come, oh miracle! and give them the burnt remains of maniocs or yams. One-eyed Kali kept on cooking meat and fish of stone and wood until the morning when the family was no longer seen in the village. Exodus, exodus, cried Souley, the local madman, to whom Old Yambo had passed the baton, and the last I heard, said Toby, the two weakest kids had died and the others were begging with their mother in the slums of the capital, where they had ended up.

Armed with a pen and two pieces of cardboard, Toby was ready to describe the rock and the wood. In his eyes, a childlike zeal, because he must still believe in his scheme, in his role as curator of a strange exhibition of junk gathered from the poor, the beggars of our savannahs. He said, For the piece of rock, I suggest, to keep it simple, "The rock for the supper of one-eyed Kali and her children." —Why not? You're improving. —You're telling me! —Could you at least put on a show of modesty? But there's no verb in your caption. The verb is action, life. What if you wrote "Every night, Kali put this rock on to roast for her kids' supper"? —Sold! I'll take it. Let's go on to the piece of wood. —How about "Some nights, this piece of wood replaced the rock in Kali's stove?" —Not bad, not bad. That way, we're making a connection between the two elements. You have talent, Robinson. Although I had my doubts. —Screw you, Toby! Now, let me go! —Ah! I almost forgot! Souley the madman brought me the wood and the rock a week after Kali and her kids left the village. —Why did he give them to you? —That's what I asked him. And can you imagine his answer? —The answer of a madman or a wise man: Why not? —No. He said, Toby, you're the first person I've run into this morning, I'm just coming from Kali's house and this is all that remains of the one-eyed woman.

4

I DIDN'T KNOW WHERE I STOOD anymore, the rope on my wrists had loosened and might give way any minute. But did I have any desire to get out of this place? The sound of cymbals, drums, and trumpets filled the air, apparently a stray marching band was passing by on the street, which must be open to traffic again. It was a brief diversion that I supposed would gradually come to an end as the band moved away from the museum. I closed my eyes on a last image of Toby transformed into a statue in the midst of the broken frames and torn photographs, figuring that the brassy clamour of the cymbals, the blare of the trumpets, and the booming of the drums would fade to silence in a couple of minutes. I whispered hesitantly, *Decrescendo, decrescendo*, the band will be drowned out by the din of the city. But no, the sound did not diminish, instead it swelled, and after what was a chaotic prelude of crazy notes and the rubbing of metal against metal, I heard the first verse of a well-known children's song:

> *In the woods nearby, there are violets*
> *Oleander, bougainvillea . . .*
> *I tied my bouquet with a strand of straw*
> *I tied my bouquet with a strand of willow . . .*

In the street, the music got louder, the violets, oleander, and bougainvillea rained down on our heads. Night was falling, and we were lulled and transported by the song, which little by little swallowed up all other sounds, the murmurs of birds, car engines, and humans. The band stopped in front of the doors of the museum, probably to mark the commemoration of an event or some festival on a calendar unknown to me; an explosion of notes made the walls vibrate, while Toby took refuge in absence. The rope holding my wrists had come undone, and since Toby had his back to my corner, I hurried to free myself from the one around my ankles. That was accomplished in a flash, but I remained there, unable to get up, my eyes fixed on Toby's back, which was more and more blurred by a mist the source of which I couldn't determine, or were my eyes playing tricks on me? The band continued its performance with a series of low notes that shook the foundations of the building and high notes that made walls and bodies tremble. 6:14, I read on my watch. The flames of Toby's lamps were burning low, my jailer was now indifferent to the commotion around us, the sounds, the violets, the oleander, and the bougainvillea still raining down. I could hardly hear him speaking, my eardrums were overheated by the music, but I managed to make out his words: Those smiles on the walls, Robinson, they keep mocking me! Don't you see it?

I didn't understand what was going on in the organized chaos among the wild roses and wisps of straw and willow blown in the wind by the infernal music, I was lost, and Toby said, You're in cahoots, is that it? I should have dealt with you right away. I've failed, so clear out! If you don't want to be contaminated by that silly laughter, get out of here! He was yelling to make himself heard over the music, and by the time I understood, it was too late.

3

DO YOU THINK IT'S TOO LATE for our part of the country? Grandmother asked me that afternoon when she described what had been her last spat with her husband, his gaze hard and his body dried out by time. Grandfather, who in the twilight of his life would count his years spent in our tropics, count the duties of his pastoral charge, gospels read, hymns sung loud and clear, and prayers uttered to the heavens from dawn to dusk, count all the petitions addressed to the silence of God that he deign to ease the bitter fate of the Black people stranded on the equator. And after counting up all that, Grandfather came to the conclusion that it could not be the good Lord's fault that things had often gone awry for us. And he said to his muse that we, the Blacks of Ethiopia, the Sahara, and the shores of Lake Victoria, were too kind, too naive, too open to the four winds. Shouldn't have welcomed the first slave traders and explorers of every kind who in those cursed days dropped anchor and set their eyes drunk with greed on our coasts. King Mlapa III of Togoville shouldn't in 1884 have signed a protectorate treaty for this land with Gustav Nachtigal, who had been sent by the emperor of Prussia. And for that matter, he added, did he actually sign anything? Should have sent Nachtigal back to his town of Eichstedt in Saxony-Anhalt, sent them all back, him and the adventurers in his crew.

Grandmother had replied curtly that he understood nothing about Africa or Africans, Nothing, after a half-century and more spent here, Hans! Nothing! To us, a stranger must be treated with respect, warmth, humanity. And didn't you yourself teach that in your Bible classes? Here, a stranger is called *amedzro*, translation: a person who is wanted. We welcomed people who came from afar and we also thought they would bring something to us in return! With them, we thought we would share in the world and its knowledge. The proof is that we welcomed you! —Don't confuse me with those sharks who came, not to admire your beautiful exotic sky, but to seize your land and everything hidden under it! And now the belly of the land around us is empty! —But that's no reason to disavow what we are, Hans! —As I said, you're naive, Fania! Like all the people here, the people I've been living with for so long. These people I've devoted my life to! You want to stay true and loving, you said? But the foreigners who come to this part of the world all wear masks! They're swindlers! There's nothing more false than their smiles. —But they opened the way for you, Hans. And in the time of the Germans, weren't we a model colony, the so-called *Musterkolonie*? It was the English and the French who messed everything up. Then it was the Americans and their Green Revolution. And now it's our new masters from China and Arabia who are buying up great swaths of our lands. But does that mean we have to disavow what we are? Our embrace of the Other, the Stranger? And also, we have resisted the invader. I recall the story of Na Biema Bonsafo, the king of the Chakosi of this part of the country, who fought the invader at the end of the tumultuous nineteenth century, until wisdom prevailed. —Well, they should have kept up the struggle, Grandfather retorted. Soon, Fania, you'll inhabit that wind that will carry off the remains of your shattered lands. You'll inhabit the wind and the dust. You've understood nothing, you and all your people, Fania! And the same usurpers keep coming back, wearing new masks, while you keep your same welcoming faces.

What comes from afar is not necessarily dangerous, Hans! said Grandmother. Or do you yourself represent a previously unsuspected danger? —I'm not a foreigner, Fania, I'm not a stranger! You're getting on my nerves! —You're my man, the only one. And a great painter. —You're making fun of me. What you need are new poets who will help you to finally understand things. —But poets all end up dying too soon. When we're barely beginning to understand. —I hope you'll at least have a little land left to bury them in. —"You"? Didn't you say you're not a foreigner? —I'm tired, Fania! And they're getting close, those vultures that will devour our remains. And I can't assure you that they'll even leave our bones in the red earth of these plateaus! They'll swoop down on us, triumphant, sinking their steely beaks into our rotten bodies! They'll gobble up the heart first, because we'll be presenting our bare chests, already swelling from the heat, to the winds and their metallic beaks. They'll go on to our closed eyelids and suck out our eyes. And the living, hiding terrified in the bushes, will cover their ears so as not to hear the horrible sucking sound. Then the vultures will pierce the bellies; imagine ten thousand voracious beaks digging into the stinking skins. Some will fight over the soft flesh of the flabby pricks and breasts, leaving the hardened toes and fingers and the bones to the latecomers. And our only salvation will be if an artist crazier than the one who created us transforms us into metal figures or shapes on a canvas. Our only chance will be if the artist places us in a plastic setting that the vultures ignore. But if a smart aleck with a brush were to amuse himself by painting those damn creatures in the sky above our dead, rotting bodies, if he were to dare, then we wouldn't be out of danger, because even in a painting they wouldn't let us be! So guess what we should do now! Guess! No? We should organize one last celebration. To enjoy ourselves a bit again, because, afterwards, there won't be anything to do. Except that I've always been uncomfortable at festivities. For a long time, I thought the people painted by my master Bruegel would teach me to feel at ease. I was never able to dance, to take a spin around a dance floor, my hand holding yours. —But you're talking nonsense, Hans, Grandmother had answered. We aren't in a dance hall of your old country of Lower Saxony.

Grandmother said it was quite a memorable moment. A few months later, Grandfather gave up his worn-out missionary ghost. And we found a little piece of land in which to bury his remains.

2

6:27 PM. YOU'VE MANAGED TO GET LOOSE from your bonds, so get the hell out of here! Toby shouted as he moved towards the back of the room, where a lamp was burning down beside the bottle of kerosene. He was three or four metres from the lamp when the heavy wooden door leading out of the room burst open and fell onto another lamp, starting a fire on the floor. Toby grabbed the other bottle of kerosene, which was farther away. I ran towards him and, in my rush, I almost collided with two guys, one armed with an automatic rifle and the other with a fire extinguisher, whose contents he was spraying on the fire. I heard shouts of Hands up! Don't move! while Toby, undaunted, raised the bottle in his hand. He was holding it tight, but I managed to overpower him and wrestle it away. Another guy with an automatic rifle pulled me towards the back and the two men tackled Toby to the floor. He lay there silent, sinking deeper and deeper into some faraway place.

A guy I identified from his voice as Commissioner Shango came in with my friend Ed Kaba, who pressed me with questions on how I was, while I couldn't take my eyes off Toby, who was still being held against the cement. Shango gave an order and Toby was picked up and dragged outside, Samuel Brown was picked up and thrown into a hole, Winnie closed her heart and her belly and her sex and locked up her beautiful breasts, little Abraham promised he would take her away from Alabama when he grew up, and, while the guy with the fire extinguisher and another big bruiser armed with another red cylinder finished putting out the lamps Toby had lit, I maintained a stubborn silence, as if only through that silence could I continue to communicate with my former jailer. As he walked past me, held firmly by the policemen with his hands cuffed behind his back, he gave me a look that I read as a reproach. He was angry at me for stopping him from immolating himself. Our eyes locked, I silently told him he would have had barely enough time to burn, the fire extinguishers would quickly have erased the image of his body on fire, he would have had, not the pleasure of a heroic death, but rather very serious injuries that would have prolonged his ordeal. I asked, Do you think Shango and his men would have told the press and the world of your heroic death? Never would they have given you that gift, they would have said you had fallen on your lamp and your oil can while trying to flee, that you'd caught fire like an old rag when the special unit of the police broke through the entrance to the exhibition hall. I would have contradicted that version of the facts, but the seeds of doubt would have been planted.

And what a ridiculous idea to want to die a hero! A hero in the indifference of the white walls of an exhibition hall, victim of military thugs who are used to dealing with these situations. What if you kept that body for love and ecstasy, for an epiphany of the senses with your redhead from Savannah? A body for love and not for some damn sacrifice? Sorry for spoiling your entry into history, my friend. But supposing you had succeeded with your plan, what would have been left to us beyond the spectacle of a body engulfed in flames, the smell of burned flesh? There might perhaps have been, as in other streets of the world, a furious crowd that for a few days pounded the cobblestones chanting, Enough is enough, it's time for change! For Toby! I am Toby! conjugating the verb to be in all the forms and tenses of misery, while the military thugs—because this isn't Berlin or New York—fired indiscriminately into the angry crowd with their placards, banners, and bandannas. However, supposing they didn't want you to be forgotten, they would have put up a little plaque or a bust of some dubious metal that wouldn't even look like you and whose only company would be the polluted air, the piss of mutts, and the droppings of birds. You'll permit me to say that one could dream of a brighter future and a more glorious legacy than that. But I may be mistaken, maybe you would have liked the company of crows and pigeons roosting on the cold, boring immortality of your bust.

Or maybe, with your action, your body in flames, we would have had our revolution, and a Growers Party would be have been born out of your charred remains and become powerful and influential. The first few months, the people of the land would believe in what it advocated in Parliament, its green discourse full of humanism. But, very quickly, with compromises, renunciations, concessions, shady deals, and chicanery, the green discourse would lose its sparkle, its freshness, its bite, and the former growers would end up supporting the classic neoliberal rhetoric and practices, having become career politicians, watching the progress of their investments in the stock market with worried eyes and trembling limbs, cunningly hiding their assets where the good Lord himself wouldn't find them, while the winds of the Sahelian desert finally eroded what was left of your plaque or bust of cheap metal. Or perhaps you might have become nothing less than a holy man, Saint Toby of the Savannah, venerable grower, canonized with great pomp one day in the year 2050 of our era by Francis II, the first Black pope, who hadn't forgotten his origins as a Sahelian and son of peasants. And from then on, in the churches, at every dawn the weary angels brought, you would be asked for miracles, you would be solicited even in death, no rest for you. Becoming a saint, my friend, is not the best investment for a legacy either. But I'm so stupid! You don't believe in the god of the Vatican, so you'll miss out on sainthood too!

1

IN THE COURTYARD OF THE MUSEUM of the Green Revolution, we walked on the beautiful white gravel behind Toby and the poker-faced policemen escorting him to the paddy wagon, the metal cage waiting with its motor purring for him to get in with his aura of a man vanquished, before it would speed away through the twilight of the city. I kept silent, I barely heard my friend Ed Kaba say they were going to take me to the hospital to make sure my machinery hadn't suffered from the tension of the past few hours. I continued staring at Toby walking ahead of me, wooden, surrounded by the cops. Just when the group was about to pass through the entrance to the courtyard, Toby slowly turned his head as if in a final salute to the memory of his revolt, his eyes met mine, and he gave me a wink, as if to reassure me, There'll be another time, Robinson! And while this was happening, the music continued, the band, whose purpose was to camouflage the sound of the police assault, kept playing enthusiastically, and in the same vein as the first piece, after the violets, bougainvillea, and oleander, we were treated to birds building their nests in the flowering lilacs, a darling blonde girl, and pretty doves and partridges, as well as a martial air to celebrate the victory of the military thugs over a troublemaking cotton grower.

In my father's garden
The lilacs are in bloom (repeat)
All the birds in the world
Come to build their nests

Next to my darling,
How good it is, it is, it is,
Next to my darling,
How good it is to sleep.

When Toby had gone, I ran back to the exhibition hall. I picked up my camera from the floor and took pictures of Toby's museum, the snapshots and the pathetic items on the walls and display stands—the piece of rope from Wali the hanged man, the containers of milk and murky water, the letters and account books, the dried leaves on a piece of cardboard, one-eyed Kali's rock and her piece of wood. I wanted to take them but Ed, behind me, murmured that I couldn't, Toby's things had been confiscated for the investigation that would come. I moved quickly, because Ed said we had to leave the premises. Outside, the band had disappeared, but I still heard the music.

0

6:35 PM, THE SUN HAD FINALLY DIED. So had Samuel Brown. With Toby apprehended, I didn't want to hang around in the museum courtyard. I had also refused to be examined by a doctor, who, with an ambulance parked on the street beside the police vehicles, must have arrived a while ago. I went back to my hotel in that noisy neighbourhood where, amid the merchants' stalls on the sidewalks and the shouting of little street vendors, I had the feeling of being in the hectic heart of the world. Back in my room, I threw myself onto the bed. Lying with hands folded under my neck and eyes closed, I tried to review the movie of the past few hours, which had been the most important of my miserable existence—the confrontation with Toby, the cold, mute images on the walls, Shango exasperated, my friend Ed helpless, Toby's last glance, or rather his stealthy wink, the band, the lilacs, oleander, and bougainvillea that had fooled us—and us carrying on from the outset in the absurd role of the vanquished, a position that only a painting by a Flemish artist dead for ages could get me out of by giving me the illusion of victory.

A thousand eternities later, Ed knocked on my door. He trudged wearily to the middle of the room, lay down on the bed fully clothed—the same outfit he was wearing in the morning when I met him at the museum, Ed the dandy, impeccable blue suit and brown Italian shoes, although his necktie had become a rag clutched in his fist—while I headed to the bathroom. When I came out, scarcely revived by the shower, we silently shared the only bottle of Scotch in the vicinity, a Johnnie Walker that I'd placed on the low table in the corner of the room, where there were two armchairs of antique leather. Ed said, Phew, what a day! I'm throwing in the towel. That is, before I get officially fired. A hell of a guy, our Toby, huh? But here's the card of a guy I know. A lawyer. He's good. They call him the devil. He's a real snazzy dresser, with his perfect suit and his felt hat. You still don't want to see a doctor? I'll come back to get you in an hour, we'll go have a bite. . . . I looked at the card and I said to myself, If that's the same man, if it's Zak Bolton, there would be no paradox in the fact that the guy who worked for The Firm also defended anti-GMO activists. Because he's the devil, the game amuses him, he simply covers his tracks and reshuffles the cards. He would get bored knowing Toby was behind bars, much preferring the pleasure of seeing us poor humans compete in the arena of stupidity, seeing us bleed each other dry. If Toby wasn't demolished, he would become more active than ever for the parties in the Olympic competitions in which enraged men fight and dismember each other, with the devil sitting in a front row seat so as not to miss any of the action. As in the story of the village of Asterix and the indomitable Gauls, who were never vanquished by all-powerful Rome, the devil—or fate—would save the underdog, Toby, so that the struggle could go on for the pleasure of our watching eyes, and for other stories and novels to come. It would be very boring, very dull, if everything were to stop there with a dead Toby.

Ed left. On the bed, I was an absurdly fragile fledging. I missed Toby. And my painting, which I hadn't seen in three months. In which, for a long time, I hoped to see Samuel and Winnie with smiling faces. The painting was still an enchantment to me, my lost child's body could go to it and touch a purity that was gone from the dirty, dead streets of everyday and the hideous creatures who walked them. I could sit down beside the bagpipe player from the countryside of Flanders and dream and breathe, because I had finally learned: to be mad, to stop and breathe while an ill wind is pushing us towards the abyss, to stop halfway to the abyss and seize what remains of the fleeting beauty of the world, and what I have left, too, of my grandparents and my lover from the Uzbek plains.

Aylmer, Ottawa, Olathe (Kansas), Berlin
July 2017-December 2020

EDEM AWUMEY was born in Lomé, Togo. He is the author of five previous novels. *Descent into Night*, the English translation of *Explication de la nuit* (2013), won the prestigious Governor General's Literary Award for Translation in 2018. His other novels are *Port-Melo* (2006), which won the Grand prix littéraire d'Afrique noire; *Les pieds sales* (2009), which was a finalist for the Prix Goncourt in France; *Rose déluge* (2011); and *Mina parmi les ombres* (2018), which was translated into English as *Mina Among the Shadows* (2020). *Dirty Feet* (2011), the English translation of *Les pieds sales*, was selected for the Dublin Impac Award. *Descent into Night* and *Mina Among the Shadows* were translated by Phyllis Aronoff and Howard Scott. Edem Awumey lives in Gatineau, Quebec.